TON BROOS

Sunken Red

Sunken Red

Jeroen Brouwers

Translated from the Dutch by
Adrienne Dixon

NEW AMSTERDAM
New York

Copyright © 1981 Jeroen Brouwers

Translation copyright © 1988 Adrienne Dixon

First published in the United States in 1988 by
NEW AMSTERDAM BOOKS
171 Madison Avenue
New York, NY 10016

Originally published in Holland as *Bezonken rood* by
Uitgeverij De Arbeiderspers, November 1981

Library of Congress Cataloging-in-Publication Data

Brouwers, Jeroen.
[Bezonken rood.   English]
Sunken red / Jeroen Brouwers ; translated from the Dutch by
Adrienne Dixon.
p. 132 cm. 32 × 48-1/2.
Translation of : Bezonken rood.
ISBN 0-941533-19-0
PT5881.12.R65B4913   1988
839.3′186409—dc19   88-19502
[B]   CIP

Printed in the United States of America.

This book is printed on acid-free paper.

*The publishers are grateful to the
Foundation for the Promotion of the
Translation of Dutch Literary Works
for bringing this book to their attention.*

Sunken Red

*Er aber, in seiner gewöhnlichen Art, hüllte sich in
Geheimnisse, indem er mich mit grossen Augen anblickte
und mir die Worte wiederholte:*

Die Mütter! Mütter! 's klingt so wunderlich!
—Johann Peter Eckermann, *Gespräche mit Goethe*

*Seek me while I am here. Know me because I am here. I
am here!*

And yet it is certain that I am not here."
—*"Song of the Dead" (South Celebes)*

"The wind, which settles only now and then, since it is always on its way from somewhere and to somewhere else, and never constantly in one place, carries in gusts, refreshing or unrefreshing, odors and sometimes a cloud of butterflies or dragonflies, but sometimes, too, a flock of blackbirds—and when it has gone again, everything in the garden, everything that can move and has been touched by it, still moves for a long time."

This mysterious sentence I found in a notebook that is more than ten years old. I never found a use for it in any of my writings, but now, after all these years I set it down here. I know now that this sentence is a metaphor.

It might appear in a death notice or in an obituary.

"The wind"; that is, someone's life.

"Nothing exists that does not touch something else."

For weeks the land has been shrouded in mist, mist which in places rolls itself into castles or cathedrals; an almost imperceptible moistness descends. Nothing moves, only the mist—we are in a period of grey mourning, we are halfway through the winter, end of January, beginning of February 1981.

During this time my mother died suddenly.

She might well have lived another ten years, she might have died ten years earlier.

They found her in the early morning of Tuesday, January 27, dead on the floor of her apartment in the old people's home where she had been living for some time.

I would not know how to find the place, nor do I know how she lived. I cannot remember when it was I last saw her.

She must have fallen from "the couch." She was lying on "the carpet" in front of this couch, but I do not know the interior of her room. Clearly, she had a couch. And a carpet.

When they found her she was already "cold" and "blue"; it is probable that she died on the evening of January 26. From the fact that the television set in her apartment was switched off, it was thought that her death must have occurred either before the start of the evening programs or after they had finished.

The light had been seen burning all night in her room, but no special attention had been paid to that.

She was lying on the floor with a sandwich in her hand, one bite of which was in her mouth. It was a cheese sandwich. The detail of the sandwich came to be known because one of the younger nurses in the old people's home let it slip a few days after my mother's death. She was reprimanded by the authorities for her indiscretion; she should not have mentioned the sandwich because "the relatives" might think that the home did not provide enough food for its residents, and that Mrs. Brouwers had died of starvation.

So my mother died biting into a cheese sandwich, this much can be recorded for posterity, though it cannot be established whether the bread was white or brown or if the cheese was mature or new, mild or with cumin seed.

"She died alone."

My mother survived her husband by seventeen years. His portrait stood on the television set; this I know from the houses in which she lived earlier and where I visited her from time to time. She also survived her elder son who was killed in a plane crash somewhere in the United States a few winters ago.

All that still happens among the Brouwers is dying. The tide goes out, death hangs over the house—for the hundredth time. I must hurry.

(Very infrequently in recent years my mother would phone me, but as soon as I spoke my name she would say, "I'm sorry, wrong number." I knew her voice by the tone and by her Indonesian accent. There are millions of mothers in the world, but only one of them is mine. Before I could answer she would hang up, and I left it at that. I had heard the voice of a mother who was misconnected with her son.)

("Croak croak!")

I received the news of her death by telephone, at about half-past eight in the morning: the ringing tore me away from a misty or dusky town in which I was walking, six or seven years younger than I am now. A lover was with me who said, The stable in Bethlehem, the house in Nazareth. . . . A bell rang, it was the telephone.

I stook naked and shivering by the large living-room window, the receiver at my ear and my hand on my member. (The beloved was called Liza.) The mist rested against the window pane, but I know the view from my window so well that I fixed my eyes on the line in the distance where the woods begin, as if there were no mist. In my thoughts I was in those woods; I saw myself standing there on the shore of a lake.

I thought, what was on television last night that my mother might just have had time to enjoy?

She suffered from Parkinson's disease. When she sat watching television her head and hands trembled, her mouth fell open and her tongue hung out. "It was a pitiful sight." I never saw it, because I did not want to see it.

I thought nothing more—which is not the same as,

I did not think of it any more. It would be better to write, I *felt* nothing.

I did not jump into my car to drive to my dead mother. I did not want to be so cowardly, after not having driven to her these last years when she was still alive.

Nor did I attend her cremation a few days later.

Lying in a coffin in the basement of the old people's home, my mother wore her "best dress." It was—it was described to me in detail—a dress in blue and soft mauve shades shot through with a little beige, not exactly flowered but with a cloudlike pattern.

In the coffin she was wearing "her glasses," of which I could form no mental picture, since I had not known that my mother wore glasses.

The "blue" had gradually faded from her face, she also seemed to become "more beautiful" every day and even "younger," she lay there as if she were "asleep."

She looked "peaceful," her hands joined on her breast.

Some members of the family thought that a rosary ought to be twined around her fingers, others thought not.

In the days between my mother's death and her cremation I searched in all my bookcases for a little book which at that time I was sure I had but which I appear to have no longer. I must have moved too often, losing books and gradually growing cynical, no longer caring about books, too often burning too many things from my past, supposedly because I was unsentimental, supposedly out of disgust for that past.

The book is *Danny Goes on a Trip,* written by Leonard Roggeveen. "Look who goes there. It is Danny. . . ."

I wanted to remember my mother by the best thing she ever gave me: from that now-lost little pre-war book, stained, smudged, crumpled, torn, my mother taught me to read. In the East Indies, in the Japanese camp, in the early forties. I was given that book on my fifth birthday.

Seated at my desk, at the moment when two hundred kilometers away my mother vanished into the fiery furnace, I would have wished to read aloud from that book, in her honor, to pay her homage in the way I thought right.

My mother always had so much courage, they all said as they stood around the coffin. Her indestructible optimism, her cheerfulness, her ready laugh.

They won't be able to say any of that about me. I am not optimistic, I am not cheerful either, and if I laugh (this is true) in the way my mother always used to laugh, something very funny must have happened or been said. In that respect I am not like her. Nor do I have her courage. On the contrary, I am really rather fearful—or worse; there are times when I am half-crazy with fear (of *undefined* things, which *suddenly* "threaten" me). Sometimes my anxiety is so great that it seems as if my face has become liquid, pulpy, and is dripping down in blobs. When the attack of anxiety is over it is as if I have a different face, and I won't be able to recognize my own reflection.

The anxiety-and-emotion-relievers I take have poetic names, such as "Seresta Forte." The pharmaceutical industry has arranged it so that one side effect of this group of drugs is that when the pill has worn off, the user is assailed by new anxieties that are caused by the drug itself. And so you become addicted to your anxiety and stay inside the grey labyrinth.

Let us pray.

With the receiver at my ear, one hand on my penis, I thought: I learn that my mother has died when I am just as naked as I was when I was born of that mother, almost forty-one years ago. By literary criteria it is trash, but I did think it.

I began to tremble all over, and not from cold. Nor from emotion or grief. Some of those who have died in my lifetime are people whom I have loved more than I loved my mother. What had seized me was *anxiety*.

I sat down on the couch by the window and reached for the plastic pill box beside the phone on the window sill.

Seresta Forte relieves anxiety and trembling. This drug may affect your driving. A pill like that takes you out of yourself, your brain-apparatus is covered up or screened off as if by condensed wads of mist. You enter into a state of unconsciousness in which you somehow remain sleepily aware even though, after a few minutes, thought is no longer possible: perhaps that is the state you were in as a small child.

You can also take fifty pills at once and, to be absolutely sure of everlasting anxiety-free unconsciousness, wash them down with a whole bottle of gin: the "tragic" death has occurred, suddenly at his home in Exel in the Achterhoek, of the author of *The Sunken*.

After I had unscrewed the lid, the trembling of my hands scattered the contents of the pill box all over me. I managed to trap some of the pills in the dip between my hastily closed thighs, where they fell on my genitals; the rest danced away in all directions over the red tiles and the carpet.

I did not take a handful of pills; I took just one. I stood up and went to the kitchen to wash it down not with gin but with water. My time has not yet come, and I certainly have no desire to make the great crossing with my mother, holding her hand.

A moment later I was standing by the living room window again. I felt peace and indifference descending on me. I saw that I had already been taken out of myself: on the other side of the window, less than a yard away, stood my other, fear-tormented self; at any rate there was a naked man standing out there in the mist, whose face consisted of something viscous, pulp-like, that trickled down from him. This person looked me straight in the eye as long as I looked him straight in the eye. When our eyes strayed away, mine fixed themselves on the patch of hair under his belly and I smiled, for what I saw could be called more or less funny. A few white pills had got into his pubic hair and were stuck there.

Simultaneously he and I took a few steps back, and I saw him retreat on the other side of the window and vanish in the mist.

When I was six or seven years younger than I am now, "I found myself in a dark wood, for I had lost the right road." My life consisted of drifting about, always half-drunk, out of disgust with life and a desire not to live.

One summer evening, in a café in the town of *** where I had fetched up by chance, I met Liza, or Liza met me. She had a friendly, gentle, intelligent face, she was wearing pastel gauzy garments that rustled at every movement she made.

"Shall we go to bed now?" I said that in less than an hour's time, or Liza said it. That was the casual language of those years, after "the revolution," the language of utter boredom, bitterness and disillusion.

I stayed with her for two or three days, then I was on my way again, in my car, alone, looking˙ for something, forgetting Liza, forgetting everything about her, even her name. But once in a long while the little town would come into my mind, decked with flags and pennants, greenery, flowers, carpets and wayside shrines.

There is no longer any question of drifting and fetching up someplace or other. I have found shelter and the other day my wife gave birth to a daughter, more or less at the moment when, not present at the birth out of aversion, I looked into the mirror and, in my anxiety, could not recognize my face. I saw the skin of my scalp shimmering through what had been my thick shock of hair, and noticed white streaks in the hair that remained. It won't be long until, when I look in the mirror, I shall see my father's portrait as it looked out at my mother for seventeen years from its place on the television set.

All the props and stage sets are in place. My life has almost come to the end of the second act, just before the intermission. I watch anxiously to see that all this scenery stays in place; if any part of it falls, it will all fall and crush me.

About a month before my mother's death, around Christmas, I was back in the town of *** and after all those years I met Liza again, or Liza met me. I was at a party, she was suddenly there, in the same room as I, full of laughing, drinking people. The moment I saw her was the moment she saw me. I recognized her with my whole body; somewhere in my head a projector was switched on, and in two seconds the film I thought I had completely forgotten was played back to me. Through the crowd of festive guests, Liza came towards me as if through a town decked with fluttering flags (Liza smiling; Liza at the window of her apartment, staring—she lives above a clock shop; Liza naked and how I caress her; Liza walking along in a procession, everything in color, a small, unimportant event in my life, but six or seven years later it caused a rumbling backstage and I saw the set totter).

While my face was still smiling I felt a great sorrow, fed by regret, arise in me—at my carelessness years ago, at those years themselves that were so full of emptiness, and at myself because I am the way I am.

We've both grown older, we said to each other. But she is still years younger than I.

The rustling of her clothes and the sound of her voice.

You've become quite a celebrity since then, she said to me. Yes, I said.

Where's your little bell? she asked, with that laugh of hers. Gone, I said. I go soundlessly through life these days. And you?

What about me?

Are you still a school teacher? Yes, she was still a school teacher.

Nothing else has changed, we said of each other, although this was clearly not true. As for my not having changed, I have changed completely; I still live in the same body which is at the same time *no longer* the same body.

Little bell?

In the days when Liza and I first met each other, I wore, at the bottom of my right trouser leg, on the outside of the ankle, a tiny silver bell, just like that, look-tinkle who-tinkle goes-tinkle there-tinkle, Danny on the chase.

I am not like that any more. Those trousers wouldn't fit me any longer in more than one respect.

We didn't say much else, but it was clear that we

thought the same thing (Tower of David, Tower of Ivory, House of Gold, Gate of Paradise) and that we would only have needed to say the same thing to each other as years ago, to take each other by the hand and leave the party and. . . .

But I am tired of the dramas that used to be enacted on my stage.

"The best thing two people can wish for each other is that they won't fall in love with each other." (Me, in an interview.)

But nothing exists that does not touch something else.

Why is it that I am the way I am?

In the days after my mother's death I thought both of my mother and of Liza, with the same passionate dispassion: reluctant to feel grief for the one and love for the other and sometimes having both those feelings at once. Those thoughts and feelings irritated me and made me afraid. They disturbed me in my work (I was writing a book about suicide in Dutch literature; I was working on the chapter about the Dutch writer, Jacob Hiegentlich, who killed himself); and at mealtimes (I could not swallow a morsel for sighing), and in my sleep (I dreamt of both women, sometimes at the same moment in the same dream).

Leave me in peace. I am not here. Make no demands on me.

I *feel* nothing and I *want* to feel nothing.

In the mist. Written in a trembling hand. Death does not concern me. Life does not concern me. Let me, too, die alone—what does it matter, for God's sake?

In those days, in the silence of my house, I sometimes pressed the telephone receiver against my ear and called out as loudly as I could into the buzzing tone:
"Croak croak!"

I hardly knew my parents, this too I have already recorded; the going-out-of-business sale of my life is almost finished, my work will soon be done. Let me not pretend to be more cynical than I am, and certainly not more sentimental either—but at least I knew my mother *then,* in those war years in the Japanese camp where she taught me to read.

The camp was called Tjideng. It was the camp of a much-feared, a notorious Japanese commandant, Captain Kenichi Sone; in 1946 he was executed as a war criminal. I remember him. He personally beat my mother and kicked her with his spurred boots and I personally witnessed it.

"She was queenly." "They struck my mother until she lay as if she were dead." "My mother was the most beautiful mother; at that moment I ceased to love her." I have recorded that, just as I have recorded, "When she dies, I won't go to her funeral."

The women's camp at Tjideng, where small boys under ten years old were also accommodated and where I lived with my grandmother, my mother and my sister, was a part of Batavia closed off by rush fencing, watch-towers and barbed wire. In the brick houses, thousands of interned European women lived with their children in spaces of a few square meters each, measured out with a ruler, which they were prepared to defend with their blood if necessary. Even the windowsills of those houses were inhabited, even the doorsteps, every individual step of the stairs, the verandahs, the corridor. Even the air in those houses was inhabited—anyone who had a hammock lived among the ubiquitous washing lines festooned with worn, drab garments.

In one of those houses, number 7 Tjitarumweg, we lived with about ten other people in the kitchen; our home was the kitchen cabinet. My mother slept on the flat work surface on top and my grandmother, my sister and I slept below, inside the cabinet—my grandmother on the shelf that divided the inside into an upper and a lower half, my sister and I on the floor beneath her.

Hunger, sickness, suffering, death. And all the rest of it.

The history of these Japanese camps threatens to be forgotten, because those who were there have kept silent about them and those who have broken the silence have done so too late, after their indignation and their hate had softened or faded, and they had already died the death that is called mildness.

I have never known those who lived through that hell to speak of the Japanese camps in a tone other than one of *affection* and even of *nostalgia,* and that may have contributed to the impression outsiders have that "it couldn't have been all that bad." The literature about the Japanese camps is scant, and consists mainly of understatements, because the writers were afraid of tears and pathos.

Alas, *I* cannot write such a camp history, even though I too have my Tjideng behind me. I do not shrink from pathos and I am not ashamed of tears, but in those days I was a self-centered, lively little boy; I never went hungry (because my mother, kindly pelican, let me peck from her rations), I was never ill, I did not suffer. I do know about death in those camps though, and about much else besides. But I can hardly claim the right to speak of that. I mention it here for a different reason, let us say for reasons of musical pitch.

In a four-volume work entitled *Oppression and Resistance, the Netherlands in Wartime,* one chapter, all too brief, is devoted to "The Japanese Occupation of Indonesia." The author of this chapter is D. M. G. Koch.

I read: "In the notorious camp at Tjideng, ten thousand women were interned, including the wife and daughter of the Governor General."

The Governor-General concerned was A. W. L. Jonkheer Tjarda van Starkenborgh Stachouwer—a triptych of a name.

My mother was called Henriette Maria Elisabeth van Maaren and she was the mother of Jeroen Brouwers and she too was interned in that camp at Tjideng. When, after several years, she was released, she was not the same as when she went in.

My mother was thirty-five, thirty-six, thirty-seven years old at the time; she had been married for more than twelve and a half years; she had three sons and a daughter.

Her husband was at that time a prisoner of war in Japan, her two oldest sons were more than ten years old and were in men's camps elsewhere in Java (so it turned out later; all that time my mother did not know where her husband and her older children were, nor even if they were still alive).

My grandmother, my mother's mother, the wife of the great composer Van Maaren, was in poor health. Towards the end I only remember her lying on her shelf in the kitchen cabinet, thinner, yellower, more blotchy every day; colder every day, too, though the sun was pounding outside and the heat came beating down. At night my sister and I had to sleep with her in turns, to keep her body warm, but she did not make it till the end; like her composer husband she died in a Japanese camp.

Suddenly my mother lost her only daughter as well: my sister contracted dysentery, and because of the risk of infection was removed to what was called the camp hospital, a place where anyone who entered was more likely to come out dead than alive. (My sister got better. In 1945, when she was eight, the dress that she had worn when she was four still fitted her.)

I was taken away from my mother, too, or my mother was taken away from me. I was the last thing she still had, just as she was the last thing I still had. I was not aware of it, then.

The *very* last thing we had was our own life. That must have been less important to my mother, and I had not yet lived long enough to know what life is.

Among the techniques of psychological torture used by the Japs at Tjideng were the periodic but always unexpected raids, during which all male children, who did not, therefore, really belong in the women's camp, were taken out of their houses and separated from their mothers. These little boys, of whom I was one, were conducted out of the camp in a long line and taken elsewhere, sometimes for days, while rumors were spread among the women that the little boys had been shot or taken by sea to one of the other islands in the Indonesian archipelago where there was said to be a separate camp for boys under ten, "the children's caravan."

I remember nothing of these expeditions, except perhaps that we boys were simply "put to work" weeding blades of grass from among paving stones somewhere, or I remember that bits of firewood had to be gathered, or that cockroaches had to be caught—in other words, that we had to do "children's jobs,"—but I also seem to remember sitting on the knee of a Japanese soldier and being allowed to take a drag at his cigarette.

What I certainly do remember is being torn from my mother like an unripe fruit not picked but ripped from its branch, so that all the leaves on the tree rustle restlessly.

In those camp years I wore an old topi that had belonged to my famous grandfather. Adorned with his headgear I paraded through Tjideng. Look-who-goes-there.

If you met a Japanese on your way through the camp, you had to stand at attention and bow. To this compulsory tribute I voluntarily added my own: I took off my topi with a flourish and said in a bold voice: *Tabé tuan*. If I did this while I was holding my mother's hand, bowing my head to the dusty road surface together with her as the soldier passed, she always reacted with an angry tug at my arm or, when the ceremony was over, with a smack on my head that sent the topi flying.

It was this topi, bobbing along amid the heads of the other little boys who had been separated from their mothers, that told my mother even at a distance that I was among the returning children. I was never *not* among the returning children. Always, in situations of chaos, marches, roll-calls, jostling crowds in which I got lost, my mother found me again, thanks to my hat.

I even took off my hat to my mother when I met her, when she and I had found each other again: *Tabé nyonya*. I never failed to find my mother again, among the thousands of mothers of whom only one was mine.

Everything that happened left me untouched, then. Everything that happened seemed inevitable and self-explanatory, as things are in the life of a small child.

I also took off my hat to my mother to wave goodbye when, after a raid, the caravan of little boys began to move off. I remember that on one of those occasions, when she had walked some way beside the column, calling out all kinds of advice to me, she was stopped by a Japanese soldier and made to stand at attention, immobile, by the side of the road. I can still hear now what she called out to me, that I must be *careful,* that I must make sure to come back to her, that I must not lose my name tag. I still see her standing there with that fellow beside her, his bay-onetted weapon pointed at her; she is so thin she looks like a skeleton covered with skin—in 1945 she weighed rather less than 90 pounds—she is wearing a torn dress and a flower-printed scarf around her head, out of shame, to hide the fact that her hair had been shorn by the guards.

I see myself, too, and what I was wearing. A jump suit with big red, blue, red-blue, purple dots, a gar-ment I wore all during that time in the camp and that I would recognize, I am sure, if I had to search it out in a pile of cast-off rags as high as the highest mountain in Java. Apart from this jump suit (in Malay it is called *tjelana monyet,* monkey pants) I wore nothing, no underclothes, nothing on my feet. Only that topi, which was the size of my grandfather's enormous pate so that my entire head could be housed inside the

31

crown. The distance between my mother and me grew at each step I took, and my mother finally disappeared. The line of boys had turned a corner, the line of boys had left the camp and the rush gates were closed, but before she disappeared I had taken off my hat to wave to her. Bye, bye-bye, tabé mamma!

It dates from that time, almost forty years ago now, that my mother and I, as long as we continued to meet and say goodbye to each other, sealed our leave-taking with one special Malay valediction. As a little boy of four or five, I used to take off my hat, as I looked back once more at my mother who stayed behind by the side of the road while I was jostled and pushed along by the little boys around me, and shouted at her as loudly as I could: *Ketemu lagi!*

The words "ketemu lagi" I had heard from the mouth of Itih, our nursemaid, when, weeping, she said goodbye to us before my mother disappeared into the truck that was to take her and her youngest children to the camp.

A look of astonishment crossed my mother's face when she heard me shout those words at her—they were far too solemn, far too pert, from the mouth of a small boy. But then she laughed, so that I knew for the rest of my life that if I said "ketemu lagi" my mother would laugh.

The words mean more than "farewell." They mean, may you prosper and be happy wherever you go.

They became sacred, incantatory code words be-

32

tween my mother and me, who said goodbye to each other hundreds of times until a few years before her death, because we were both like the wind that seldom stays, being always on the way from and to somewhere else. And until the last few times, when we said these words to each other we laughed, although in the end we did so only with our eyes and it would have been more fitting if, just for once, we had wept.

The same story, in a different key.

After the war, having been repatriated to the Netherlands, I disappear almost at once, for the rest of my childhood, into monastically run boarding schools, because my camp experience and other events in post-war Indonesia have made me "wild," I have "no moral sense," I have no "feeling" for what is "right" and what "isn't right," and I recognize no authority.

(Indeed, in those days I was immensely happy: never afraid, never a prey to doubt, never sad.

They should have left me like that. I would have become pope or prime minister at the very least, and my parents would have been *proud* of me.)

When I am handed over to the boarding school, my mother wears a grey sombrero kind of hat with a little veil that has been resting on the hat brim, a veil that falls in front of her face as she bends down to kiss me goodbye on my mouth. This incident is characteristic of the rest of my life: we kiss each other through a barrier of spider-web.

The barrier between me and treacherous woman-kind has never been lifted since; hatred for my mother has marked my view of life from that moment on.

I must be *obedient*. In five weeks' time I will come home for the weekend and that five weeks will soon pass. I must not lose my wallet—it has important personal papers in it (certificate of baptism, identity card, coffee-ration coupons, sugar-ration coupons).

Ketemu lagi, Mamma!

I take my place in the line of pupils who bump into me when the order to march has been given, an order which I have understood too late. I look at my mother on the edge of the playground, under chestnut trees which I shall find standing in all the playgrounds of all boys' boarding schools. Laughing (the way she could laugh) she exchanges a few words with the friar who has given us the order to march. The friar has a yard-long rosary hanging from the cord around his waist. I reckon you can give a hefty whack with such a rosary. I do not understand the difference between a Japanese camp guard and a friar. Nor do I understand the difference between this column in which I walk willy-nilly, anno 1950, ten years old now, and the column in which I walked scarcely five years ago, also away from my mother—but then still wearing my hat by which she could immediately recognize me among the other little boys, while now I am no longer wearing that hat and can tell from the way her eyes scan the column that she can no longer distinguish me from the other boys. I do, however, understand the difference between this mother and the mother of scarcely five years ago. This mother betrays me.

Why didn't they beat her to death in the Jap camp?

Year in, year out, my mother and I say goodbye to

each other in windy stations as the train screeches to a halt, as the train begins to move off with me in it, as the train rumbles out of the station into the darkness and immediately describes a curve so that my mother, standing on the platform waving her handkerchief, disappears at once behind the clacking wheels.

We call something to each other that no one else understands.

We laugh.

I don't give myself away.

Danny goes on a trip.

The years wear on. My mother no longer sees me off at the station.

My parents have gone to live in a house behind which the railway runs. From the passing train, for less than a second, I can see my mother standing in the lamp-lit window on the upper floor, waving a towel. But I don't even bother to raise my head. I am reading.

Let her die, the old crone, who salves her sentimental conscience by waving at me from ever greater distances with ever larger pieces of cloth.

Among the clean clothes in my suitcase she has slipped kilo bags of toffees, packets of biscuits and bars of chocolate—exactly as I, later, can think of no other way to delight the children of my first marriage, whom I deserted, than by stuffing banknotes into

36

their hands before they once again vanish from my life for several months, thank God.

Where, when, from whom should I have learned to feel?

To me, my mother was already dead; from that moment on I never really thought of her in earnest.

Every year around her birthday I transferred a sum of money into her account, and that was that.

I repaid her for those toffees, and for teaching me to read I repaid her by writing books which she could have read. But just as she—rightly—never thanked me for the money I sent her, so she never read a single line written by me, and that was that, too. She preferred crossword puzzles, and I never blamed her for it.

All this leave-taking finally broke forever all communication between my mother and me, and I learned to live with the barrier between me and her and between me and the others. My love is lost.

As for the death notice that was sent out after my mother's death, I asked that my name not be mentioned among those of her children. It is true that she was my mother. It is true that she was not my mother. She was in my life like the wind: sometimes touching me, but mostly not present.

What if she had phoned me that evening before she died. Perhaps I would have gone to her, if she had asked me. Perhaps I would have prepared that cheese sandwich for her, and perhaps, when she fell from the couch, I would have caught her in my arms, and perhaps. . . .

But it did not happen that way, as so many things do not happen, and something else happens instead.

To hell with her.

I mean, to hell with all mothers.

On the evening my mother died, I had a visitor. A writer. (For those who are curious, for the record, that writer was Ger Verrips.) We talked about literature and politics. Mostly we talked about the Writers' Union—why I did not want to be a member of it, and how that disinclination could be explained by my asocial and paranoid character. I don't need anyone and I don't want to need anyone. I prefer to do everything myself. I regard four-fifths of the members of that Writers' Union as not being my colleagues. I want to write something instead of wasting my time with nonsense. Leave me in peace, because wherever I am nothing remains untouched, and unrest and commotion arise.

When my guest had gone, the television programs on Netherlands 1 and Netherlands 2 were already over, but on Germany 1 there was still a feature film in progress: *Kumonosuyo,* "The castle in the forest of spider webs," a Japanese version of the Macbeth story, directed by Akira Kurosawa.

I stared absentmindedly at the screen, not really trying to follow the plot, but when I did pay attention I felt irritated: those barbarous Krauts had dubbed the Japanese dialogue in German.

The fate of the Japanese German-speaking Macbeth in this film version was the same as that which befell Kenichi Sone, the commandant of Tjideng:

> A sigh can be heard—
> the swish of the cleaving sword
> as it parts the air.
>
> The criminal wears
> a sudden collar of blood.
> He loses his head.
>
> As red as the head
> sinking down in the soft mud
> is the rising sun.

(Who were "worse" in the war, the Germans or the Japanese? And which camps were more gruesome, the German or the Japanese?

No surviving victim has ever spoken of the German camps with affection and nostalgia. Those who survived the German camps did not laugh at them in the way that ex-prisoners of the Japanese laughed at the Japanese camps, supposedly to make a relative matter of what cannot be made relative.

The servants of death spoke German and they spoke Japanese too. Sometimes I hear on television how the servant language of one civilized nation is replaced by the servant language of the other, and I observe: the Jap speaks German—just as it can be imagined that in Japan the language of the Kraut is dubbed in Japanese.

Death doesn't care what language his servants speak.)

As the film went on and I sometimes watched and sometimes didn't, waiting to grow sleepy, I busied myself removing calluses from the soles of my feet: first with a rasp, then with a coarse file, then with a fine file.

Once every so many months this act of hygiene has to be performed because the horny crusts, apart from causing an unbearable itch that cannot be cured in any other way, tear holes in socks and even in sheets.

As the advancing forest came nearer and nearer to pay Macbeth what was due him, the grated skin rustled down from my feet and formed an ever-thickening layer of greyish floury powder on the newspaper spread out under my feet (*de Volkskrant* of January 26, 1981. "Mao's widow receives death penalty. Stay of execution granted").

I took the paper into the garden to throw away the collected filings. I threw them into the air the way the ashes of a cremated body are thrown into the air so that the wind will scatter them, but the powdery debris fell back to earth at once—there was no wind to take it away or even to touch it. Part of it landed on my face and stuck to my forehead, cheeks and eyelids.

41

In the fields around the house, banks of mist piled against and on top of one another. It was a sluggish Dutch winter night, not cold and not not-cold. If it hadn't happened to be night it could equally well have been day. At this time of year in this part of the world, the day is as grey as the night and the view is the same, a moistness comes down from the sky for weeks on end, invisible and inaudible in the day as it is in the night; the silence is profound.

The trees, shrubs and hedges in my garden, forming the boundaries between my world and the other worlds, between me and hundreds of other writers, between me and the readers of my books, stood like stage props in their places, motionless, they allowed themselves to be wrapped in mist. Like Macbeth I did not believe that this scenery would ever begin to walk.

During those few seconds in my garden I thought of Liza in her dragonfly-blue transparent garment, years earlier, and of Liza as I had seen her barely a month ago. Hallowed be thy name. Blessed art thou. Among women.

I thought of her standing at that very moment by the window in the town where she lives. The town lay under a dome of mist, but she knew its contours so well that she could follow the line of the narrow little streets with her gold-colored eyes just as if there were no mist. Where she and I had walked, both of us equally drunk, or half-drunk, and both of us uncommittedly and yet divinely lusting for each other. Look-tinkle-who-tinkle-goes-tinkle-there. Where we, in those narrow streets before reaching her apartment, had leaned against each other in close embrace, for a bit of kissing, a bit of nibbling, a bit of stroking, together with saying words that were ages old. The way the town was decorated. Flowers. Flags. Where she had said, in that town: this is the stable in Bethlehem, this is the house in Nazareth. . . . To which I gave a scornful reply that consisted of hearty frog's croaks.

(I am "not nice." I am so "hard" and "bitter." I am so "unfeeling." By the time she started saying this, as all the people in my life eventually do, I would be gone.

What was this Liza to me?)

(I am sitting on my water-lily leaf and collect so much air that my throat and cheeks bulge and my head turns the color of blood. Kiss me. I am a prince disguised as a frog. Sometimes I throw out my tongue like a harpoon to devour a dragonfly that rustles like cellophane between my jaws as I grind and swallow it.)

In my imagination I saw her in the rectangular lamplit window above the clockmaker's shop window, as if on a television screen. She was in her nightgown but she could not sleep, she was restless, she was thinking of me as I was thinking of her, she whispered my name. Her nightgown was of a delicate blue and a delicate mauve and it was transparent—but alas, the window sill was just a little too high for me to see her holy, as if gold-painted triangle, and at the top the frail garment was all flounces and frills and her long girlish hair hung down over it so that her breasts were not visible either. But as this dream-Liza raised the net-curtain with one hand, I saw the golden down under her arm.

For one split second I imagined that I was with Liza in her bedroom. I tore the gauzy garment away from her and slid into her body as I had done years before, carelessly opening her up by pressing her knees down on either side of her lovely face. What matters here is the word "carelessly." At each thrust I administered to her, she and I called out in turn to the Holy Virgin: Spiritual Vessel, Sacred Vessel, Precious Vessel of Godliness, Mystical Rose, Tower of David, Tower of Ivory, House of Gold. . . . Pray for us. Pray for us. Croak! Croak! Then I exploded in a flash of dazzling white light and vanished in the ticking and humming of a hundred clocks.

Later I thought that in this split second my mother may have died.

Standing amid my motionless stage scenery I sucked in lungfulls of mist. I folded the newspaper eight times. I went back into the house, I heard my wife's breathing. I heard my daughter's breathing.

I have reached the age at which immobility begins.
Life, love, literature and death—they do not con-

cern me any more. It is too late now, I have reached my destination, it is almost finished.

I saw myself in the bathroom mirror. I saw my balding skull and the white in my remaining hair. I saw the dust of my callused feet on my face.

At Tjideng, my mother, so she told me once, lived from day to day. Each day that she stayed alive with her loved ones was a day gained. Beyond that she lived from hour to hour and finally from minute to minute.

The servants of death had ochre faces and almond eyes. The servants of death dressed in brown-green uniforms and wore brown-green caps on their lank-haired heads. The servants of death had big mouths and spoke a hieroglyphic language.

My mother, who has now met the ferryman, will have recognized the language he speaks.

Let us pray.

I have never known exactly what that is, praying. There was a time when I knew all the prayers, litanies, formulae of the Catholic faith by heart. I soon realized that the mere uttering of these texts was not "praying," but whatever ought to be added to that I did not know. I stopped thinking about it.

I have said millions of Hail Marys, but I have never *prayed* one Hail Mary.

"Prayer makes you feel peaceful," said my grand-mother.

I feel peaceful when I stare into the flames of an open fire.

Thanks to my early days at Tjideng, it is part of my "view of life" that prayer, like staring into the flames of an open fire, serves no purpose and leads nowhere.

My mother left prayer to *her* mother, who, in the kitchen cabinet in which we lived, had already assumed the posture of a saint in a reliquary of granite and wood, lying in state with a rosary of black beads in her fingers. Flowered dress. My sister and I could tell she was still alive by the movement of her thumb as she let bead after bead slide through her hand, mumbling Hail Mary after Hail Mary—pray for us sinners, now and in the hour of our death, amen.

When my mother was on a work detail, she left my sister and me with our grandmother: our grandmother to look after us, and we to look after our grandmother. My sister had to try to keep her alive by feeding her, at regular intervals, spoonfuls of a porridge called bubur, a cold, thin, starchy substance without color or taste or nutritional value, the mere sight of which made us retch, hunger or no hunger.

I fled while my sister patiently fed my grandmother. My sister looked like a little old witch disguised as a child of seven, and my grandmother let the porridge drool over her face, like a baby disguised as a dying old woman. My sister's hair was a mass of small natural curls, my grandmother wore her hair pulled tightly back in a meagre bun on her neck—my sister's hair was as grey as my grandmother's.

It was clear that my grandmother was dying. I could tell by the flies that settled and crawled over her body and face and were not brushed away.

Before I could read I knew all about death. It was so much a part of my early years to be bluntly confronted with death that as far as I knew there was no emotion attached to it, no fear, no sorrow, no revulsion.

A person who was dead was rolled into a rush mat and taken away on a handcart. Her possessions, especially if they included a crumb or grain of food, were fought over, and the place she vacated would be "tchooped" even before the corpse was removed. (To tchoop was a camp word for "take possession of," "claim.")

"Mrs. So and so is dead" was a statement like "It is raining."

I saw dead women every day: their legs gave out during the prolonged roll calls in the hammering heat in the kampulan square (the roll call square); they fell forward or backward or sideways while on work detail; they did not get up when it grew light in the morning, or they sat down or lay down in the middle of the day, closed their eyes and turned out to be dead.

That was the way it was, and it was as unremarkable as a piece of chalk falling to the ground and breaking in two.

The literal meaning of the words "dead simple."

One day Nettie Stenvert was dead. She owned a doll with eyes that could open and shut.

Holding my mother's hand I stood by the body of Nettie Stenvert who had been my friend. They had put the little corpse, with a ribbon in her ringlets, in a tea chest and covered it, all but the head, with the silvery paper that had lined the chest.

I giggled, child of five or six that I was, and my mother even made me, Holy Mary, take off my hat.

I looked at the flies that walked over Nettie's closed, almost translucent white eyelids.

All I thought was: since she's dead anyway, I'll tchoop her doll with the eyes.

For the rest I thought nothing. It would be better to write, I *felt* nothing.

I fled from the kitchen we lived in, where my grey sister was spoonfeeding porridge into my grey grandmother, because I needed air and space, which I could not get in my place at the bottom of the kitchen cabinet, where I had been crouching, hiding behind my hat. I ran away, shouted at by my worried sister— into the sun, and blinking my eyes against the shimmering light, tossing my arms about and screaming, *screaming* myself inside out. It was clear that everyone would die and equally clear that all who died would soon turn into bubur.

But I was alive. Look-who-goes-there. I would

49

even be alive when my grandmother was dead and my mother was dead and my grandfather was dead and my father and the bigger of my two brothers, and everybody. One day I would write down that I walked there, in that camp under my hat, and that I saw things there which are indescribable but which I would nevertheless have to describe.

In order to stay alive:
Every day I repeated the letters and the words my mother had taught me by writing them with her finger or a stick in the sand and at the same time in my brain—
"the," "then," "and," "hand," "on," "oen," "roen," "je-roen". . . .

Someone on whom flies settled without being brushed away by the person they had settled on, was on the way to death; it was one of the unmistakable signs. From that time, I think, dates my obsession with flies. I see them crawling in thick clusters on the sick, emaciated, bruised, bleeding or otherwise be-draggled bodies, thousands of them at once, buzzing in a thousand ways.
I saw red flies in that camp, describing lassos above or around me while the blood dripped from their wings.
On me the flies did not settle. I made sure to be on the move always: playing airplanes—running around with outspread arms, brum brum. So not only was I

always the biggest fly, the one of whom all the other flies were afraid, but I was also the biggest bomber. My hat was the cockpit and the armor-plated cupola, and I flew all over Japan to bomb its cities. There goes Danny. Ricketicketick. No fly could keep up with me and all the Japanese women that fell into my hands screamed with pain and drowned in their own blood.

During rest periods, when we were all on and inside our kitchen cabinet, I made sure I sat quietly by my mother, watching sharply so no fly could land on her while she slept. I fanned my hat back and forth above her—flies don't like wind and movement.

I was an expert at catching cockroaches, bedbugs, mosquitoes and flies, especially flies. As soon as I saw them they were dead. The mosquito nets under which we slept were stiff and stank of the bloody remains of these insects. I caught them by trapping them with one hand in the netting which I threw over them with a sudden flick, while at the same time I crushed them dead with the thumb or the knuckles of the other hand. To avoid having to hear the sound of this crushing, I made it myself, by imitating it aloud: "Tets!"

It gave me a tingling feeling in my scrotum and I squeezed my buttocks tightly together.

It was clear that everyone would die, but my mother must not die. After the camp we would all be together again, my father, my brothers, my enormous grandfather, and go back to our house with the swim-

51

ming pool in the garden, untouched, immortal, and with no memory of the Jap camps. . . .

What is left of the dead in my life?

Nettie Stenvert, would anything at all be left of her now? A fragment of bone, preserved in a lump of mud, a fragment of a curl in a crumpled bit of tinfoil?

My mother, too, would get that faraway look in her eyes when, late in the sixties, "the camp" came up in conversation, as if she were homesick for Tjideng and for those years.

"Well, we did laugh a lot there, you know."

I noticed little or nothing of that, but perhaps grown-ups laughed at times when I was asleep or when I was somewhere else.

I remember that at home, long after the war, there would be *screams* of laughter when my parents, my brothers, other relatives or friends, raked up memories from their camp years. The history of those camps has been washed away on waves of hilarity.

Hirohito, the emperor of Japan, a war criminal of the stature of Hitler—until 1945 he was worshiped as a god by his subjects—was received with full pontifical honors by the Dutch government, as a friendly head of state, about a quarter of a century after his crimes. There were protests, for instance from the cabaret artist Wim Kan, a survivor of the Japanese camps, but most of the ex-inmates of those camps had no doubt already laughed too much at their camp past: the protests were not taken seriously, they were ignored.

"People from the Indies," such cheerful, jolly people.

As I sit here writing my piece about that time in the camp, Pope Woytila is spiraling down in his airplane into Japan, where, for a few seconds, he will pull a sad face by the memorials to the victims of the atom bombs on Hiroshima and Nagasaki, before pressing ex-god Hirohito to his heart.

My father saw the giant mushroom of light on the horizon, bursting from the earth's crust as the bomb exploded on Hiroshima. As a result he is supposed to have been blind for several hours, days, or weeks. Under his left eye a wart appeared that was as big as an egg.

(I cannot vouch for the truth of this blindness, with the laughter at his camp experiences still ringing in my ears, but the quivering purple wart that bulged from his face like a small replica of the mushroom I have seen myself, and in one of the formal portraits he sat for in the course of his life one can see that the wart was removed by the photographer; in 1949 it was removed by surgery.)

Because of the bombs on Hiroshima and Nagasaki, my mother, my sister and I and thousands of other starving prisoners of war received no food or drink for three days—not even bubur was issued.

This is among my childhood memories, just as among the childhood memories of others at the age I was when I was in that camp, is the memory of having had their tonsils removed (my tonsils had already been removed).

There is much more that belonged to the assumptions of my childhood years. I saw it, it lies hidden away in the attic of my memory.

Then it left me untouched. I was not to be touched by it until much later.

Sometimes I am seized with panic: sometimes I am back in that camp.

I see the Jap beating a woman with a rattan cane, or if it is not a rattan cane it is a rifle butt. She topples to the ground, screaming and drawing a trail of blood that is sucked in by the earth and becomes invisible.

She has stolen a crust of bread. She has lit a fire to boil some water. She did not notice, or she noticed too late, a patrolling Jap, so that she did not bow or did not bow soon enough. She was late for roll call.

One woman has to stand at attention naked, in the roll call square for twenty-four hours. During the day the sky looks as if it will burst in the violent heat. At night she sings as loud as she can, in the hope that it will make her feel warm; she stands at the heart of a web of searchlights. From the watchtowers around the camp, machineguns are directed at her day and night.

One naked woman has to crawl on all fours through the streets; there is a rope around her neck that is held by the Jap who walks behind her. When she finds excrement in her path she is forced to sniff at it like a dog. The Jap strikes her on her back with a stick, and on what once were her buttocks, but are no longer, so thin is she. The Jap kicks her in the crotch with his hobnailed boot.

With a few other children I hop and skip along,

laughing loudly at the sight of the woman having her face pushed into a heap of muck. Frenziedly buzzing flies cluster on her face and shorn head and on the bleeding place between her legs where the Jap keeps kicking her.

For skipping and laughing and watching eagerly, I strike my own face to this day, whenever the atrocious scene comes back in memory. *Then* I did not know that it was atrocious and that I myself was part of the atrocity.

My camp syndrome is the remorse I have today for having been that eager, keen-eyed child.

A Jap pours water into a woman until her skinny body bulges and one can hear the water splashing inside her, the way you can hear water splashing inside a water butt. Then the Jap starts hitting her in the stomach with a stick. Then the Jap jumps on her stomach with his boots. The liquid that escapes from all the orifices of her body has every imaginable color and comes out of her in every imaginable way: splattering, rippling, trickling, in the form of vomit, of blood, of porridge.

Pray for us.

One woman is locked up in what is called "the oven": a dog kennel of corrugated iron whose roof is the anvil for the sun's hammer, and against whose red-hot walls she cannot lean or she will burn herself and will stick to them with her skin. In the only possible, wretched posture she can adopt inside the oven she is surrounded by crawling and madly fluttering insects. She is stung and sucked by these insects and she cannot chase or kill them without some part of her body touching the roof or the sides of the oven. She is condemned to immobility and patience as she slowly stews. If she does not keep her wits about her she will go mad; she listens to the humming and buzzing of the insects that come to sound like clanging bells or droning organs.

One woman has her hands tied behind her back, and then is hanged from a gallows by her wrists so that her arms are pulled out of their sockets upside down, back to front, inside out, or in still other ways. She dangles in a strange curl above the ground, turning on her axis; they let her dry out and shrivel up in the scorching sun—the sun is the cruelest instrument of torture the Japanese have at their disposal, the sun is the symbol of the Japanese nation. When the woman loses consciousness she is beaten until she comes round again, because she must endure her humiliating torment in full awareness. Anyone passing by is obliged to look at her. I often pass by.

My mother, too, was beaten, shorn, and made to stand in the roll call square for twenty-four hours. I saw her there.

Who knows what was done to her that I did not see.

In our house in the camp I go into the front room one day where Nettie Stenvert lives. Nettie Stenvert's mother is lying on her back on a table, with no clothes on, her legs up and spread out. Between her legs stands a Jap who has let down his trousers, so that I roar with laughter because this really is the funniest thing I have ever seen, though in the course of my camp years I shall see it several more times in various ways, but then I will not laugh. With jerky movements the Jap pushes himself against the table, at every jerk the table is shoved a centimeter forward, so that its legs screech on the stone floor. The Jap has one hand pressed on Mrs. Stenvert's mouth and his other on her throat, but he must release his grip to give me a whack in the face that sends my hat flying from my head and gives me my first nosebleed. At that moment, when Mrs. Stenvert begins to wail loudly, I see, all in color, that the Jap pulls something that protrudes like a long hard truncheon from his hairy belly out of a gap between Mrs. Stenvert's legs. At that very moment, crying even louder than Mrs. Stenvert, seeing stars and my hands all bloody, I begin to run, ricketicketick! tets! tets! towards the remorse and the fears of years to come.

I asked whether there was a glass cover on the coffin in which my mother lay in her best dress. So that no flies would crawl on her body, her face and her glasses.

What could there have been to laugh at in that camp?

As I write this, a "women's strike" is taking place in the Netherlands. In the Dam Square in Amsterdam women smear tomato ketchup on their crotches and lie down in the roadway on their backs, their thighs spread.

Spoiled, affluent-society bitches. What do they know?

Anyone passing by is practically forced to look at them even if he doesn't want to, and his heart thumps against his temples with revulsion at this aggressive and misplaced vulgarity and he begins to tremble all over—from fear, from anger, from "vicarious" remorse in behalf of these stupid women.

When my mother was made to stand in the roll call square for twenty-four hours, as a punishment, the monsoon was just beginning. Through the pouring rain my mother went on smiling at me; I was hiding around the corner of one of the nearby houses and I waved to her and blew her kisses—I did not get wet under my hat.

It struck me that my mother, whom I had quite often seen naked, like many other mothers, no longer had the warm, plump breasts she once had; in her thinness—and also because her hair had been shorn—she not only no longer looked like *my* mother, but she no longer looked like a mother at all, and not even like a woman. Of the person who stood there in the rain it could be said only that it was "like a human being." But she was my mother, all right.

I would have wanted to fly to her in my airplane and, tilting, with wings vertical, skim past to throw her my hat so she would at least have something to cover herself with. But by means of grimaces and one stretched-out finger she signaled that I must stay where I was, the machine guns pointed at us from all the watchtowers.

That night I stayed in my hideout. Sometimes my mother and I heard in the distance the frightened little voice of my sister who was looking for us. I wanted to stay near my mother and keep watch over her; shone upon by five or six searchlights, she stood in a focal point of light, in a cloak of rain. To stay awake I scratched the rain-softened calluses from my feet with a sharp pebble. I practised: "mo-ther." From time to time I shrieked: HailMary-fullofgrace-theLordis-withthee.

We won't ever betray each other, will we Mamma? We will never leave each other, will we? Will we? Will we Mamma?

At a time when my life still is one of "drifting" and being "washed ashore," about twenty-five years after the camp at Tjideng and thousands of kilometers away from it—I am at a garden party, it is midsummer, after midnight.

Smiled at by the girls, who at that time do not yet dream of emptying ketchup bottles into their crotches, we men shoot with rifles at a target fixed under a bright lamp in the garden. On the target, a picture of a naked woman has been painted. The bull's-eye (one thousand points!) is the black triangle where her legs join her body.

It is my turn to shoot, haha, give me that thing, I say, let me treat that poppet to the lethal pollen from my squirt.

I am in that state of drunkenness in which I am still resoundingly boisterous and the quips rise from me like bubbles of marsh gas. (The next stage is that of melodramatic gloom. The one after that is the one desired: the spirit leaves my soggy brain.)

I shoot carelessly, from the groin, as though the carbine were a revolver.

Then cheers break out, the men slap me on the shoulders, the girls press kisses on my face; what an unforgettable party; Danny, the great screwer, I scored a thousand points.

But at the moment that the bullet leaves the gun with a plop and hits the target almost simultaneously with tenfold magnified sound, I remember, some time before, elsewhere, somewhere in my life, seeing a naked woman standing in the beam of the sharp searchlight while both the woman and I knew that in the surrounding darkness guns were aimed at her.

Ding ding! Droning organs.

I know: when I die and if it is true that in the hour of death one sees one's life passing in film flashes, my film will stop briefly at *this* moment.

As if I myself were hit by a bullet, something explodes in me which had been waiting to explode for years and years.

Partly under the influence of drink, of course—let me not pretend to be "sensitive" or more sentimental than I am—I suddenly weep like a fool. A veil of sunken red comes down before my eyes.

Oedipus weeps. On his feet crusts of callus flourish, like horny shoes.

My mother waves to me with a handkerchief, with a towel, with a sheet: she vanishes. My mother wears a flowery scarf on her shorn head, between her forehead and the scarf she has stuck a loose curl, to suggest that she has not had her hair shorn: she vanishes. My mother wears a grey hat and in front of her face hangs a net of spider web so that I cannot see whether she wears glasses or not: she vanishes. My mother has no breasts, my mother looks "like a human being," she is standing in the rain, I look at the fluffy, soon-to-be-dripping hair under her belly in which the rain drops hang like transparent beads: she vanishes. My mother lies on her back and presses, out of the hole between her outspread thighs, a cobblestone, that is my head, let us pray, all that blood! Never again can my head go back through that hole. My mother laughs the way she can laugh, and waves to me, all those years, all my life, ketemu lagi!—she vanishes,

My mother and I can no longer get through to each other.

The barrier between me and treacherous womanhood.

I shoot carelessly. From the groin.

Those film flashes that my mother saw when she died
I shall see too when I die—they are flashes of the same
moments in her life and in mine.

I am one of those people who cannot be "happy";
sick with everlasting restlessness, sick with everlasting fear, preferably drowsy from pills, preferably
dead drunk, preferably asleep, preferably absent.

Now that my mother has died after all, it is as if
suddenly doors are bursting open in me that had hith-
erto been closed, and as if I must go through door
after door in order to return to some kind of beginning in the fog of my existence. But I do not want to
go through all those doors, back to the past.

Take away my memories, into the fire with them,
like my mother.

(Liza laughing. Liza at the window. Liza staring naked. Liza in a procession.

Her golden eyes. Her honey-colored hair.)

It wasn't just what I needed, seeing Liza again after all those years, I being the same as I had been years ago and at the same time *not* the same, just as Liza was the same Liza she had been years ago and yet *not*. It wasn't just what I needed, being more or less in love and more or less in mourning at the same time. Mostly, it kept me from the book I was busy writing. I was engrossed in the suicide of Jacob Hiegentlich.

I took excessive doses of "Seresta Forte," to keep myself out of myself, so as not to have to think, so as not to be seized by anxiety, not to be accompanied by anxiety. And that way you stay inside the grey labyrinth.

In those days between my mother's death and her cremation, I sat by the phone, my hand already stretched out to pick up the receiver as soon as the ringing began. I *expected* it to ring, my will and longing that it would were so strong. And my mother would phone me but she would speak in Liza's voice. "I love you. Will you come to me?"

At night, in the silence that was filled with the

breathing of my wife and the breathing of my little daughter, I slipped, scarcely breathing myself, out of the marriage bed, to slink about the house, listening, drawn helplessly to the telephone.

(In my dream I had stood by the coffin where my mother lay in her dress of blue, mauve and beige shades, "more beautiful" than when she was alive and seemingly "younger" than when she died. I bent over the glass lid under which she lay; I saw that my breath made a misty patch between my face and hers. When I had wiped the condensation from the glass with a windshield-wiper movement, I saw that it was not my mother lying in the coffin, but Liza, and then again not Liza, but Nettie Stenvert's doll with the ringlets, its eyes closed. Suddenly the glass cracked, and the cracks branched out in all directions, and then each branch forked out again, farther and farther, until a complicated, opaque network of cracks had developed through which, leaning my full weight on the glass plate, I fell into an explosion of shattering glass. As I tumbled into the bottomless-seeming coffin, falling through a never-ending black-red space, seeing myself getting smaller and smaller until finally I was no bigger than a fly, I fell into a wave of semen that burst from me and I awoke, shamefaced, like an adolescent caught in the act, his body aching with remorse.)

I dialed my mother's phone number, but out of the far away silence there came a different voice from the one I recognized as my mother's: "Hello?" . . . (Give me the right insight, give me peace.) "I beg your pardon? Hello? Who's calling? Do you know what time of night it is?"

What time of night it is.

I wanted to ask my mother whether or not they had put a rosary in her hands in the coffin, because I had not seen that in my dream.

Or I dialed Liza's number, just to hear her say her name, preferably with a little sigh, and to hear her breathe—at the sound of which my head was filled with a gale of wind. I longed so much for her, my thoughts went with such violence to her that she could not but be aware of it, somehow, hundreds of kilometers away (she suddenly stopped what she was doing, she raised her head with a snap and stretched out her hand to the phone as if she expected it to ring, she felt as if someone was blowing at her, she felt it, through her gossamer nightgown, in the soft hair under her arm). She was bound to know that it was I who had phoned her, to comfort myself with the sound of her voice and then, without having told her who I was or having said anything at all, to hang up (and: in the silence that now fell in her room again she still listened intently for some time, for it seemed to her that one of the clocks in the shop below had started ticking more slowly and more loudly).

Liza, Liza.

I could not breathe for restlessness.

At times my hands trembled so much that I could

not put my finger in a hole on the dial, or keep it there to turn the disk.

Play something for me on that instrument that brings forth crystal sounds, as of broken glass falling on broken glass, a sound as of bells tinkling, so that perhaps I may be soothed.

Or again, in the middle of the day or the middle of the night, I switched on the television whose screen, on all channels, showed nothing except the same mist that stuck to the outside of the windows of my house, and from which, as it lit up, there came a "cosmic humming."

I hoped that in the mist on the screen I would see a face, however vague, however briefly, that would look at me from the unfathomable distance and, though its eyes were sad, would smile at me.

Whose face?

My mother's. But I could not even remember her old face, nor could I picture my mother's head except on Liza's blossoming body: Liza's body was covered with breasts, Liza must be cruelly tortured, Liza must have leg after leg and wing after wing torn from her body, and to be fully conscious while she was being tortured.

Out of the cosmic humming in the television box no voice came to me, no voice spoke even one word to heal my soul.

I thought, if only the postman would bring me a

letter from Liza, *now* sealed with the imprint of her lips where she had pressed a kiss on the paper and in which she called me again, as years ago, her dear heart, her puppy, her honey-sweet, her wicked wolf and other things like that.

The postman brought me a grey-edged death announcement, with a dull red fifty-five cent stamp.

"Suddenly, today, our dearly beloved mother, mother-in-law and grandmother, Henriette Maria Elisabeth van Maaren, widow of Jacques Theodorus Maria Brouwers, aged seventy-two years."

She was my mother and she was not my mother: my name was not mentioned in the death notice.

The town of ***, through which Liza and I wandered hand in hand that night, years ago, on the way to her bed above the clock shop, was decorated in such a way that I reacted by croaking like a frog, to express my nausea and revulsion.

Lengthwise above the streets they had stretched a gold-colored rope on which, every so many steps, a ball that looked like a bead had been strung. This "string of beads" ran through the entire town center and represented, Liza said, a rosary. Croak!

Two days later, on a Sunday, in keeping with an old tradition, a procession of the Blessed Virgin went through the streets, following the path of the beads, under each of which a Hail Mary was said. Prelates, parish priests, nuns, friars, altar boys and brides. Floats, banners, candles, palm branches, bells and brass bands, censers, baldaquins. Biblical and historical pageants. The golden monstrance containing "Our Lord." The ancient miraculous oaken statue of the Virgin, decked out in silk, lace and ermine. At some street corners and squares the procession paused briefly at one of the wayside altars set in cardboard shrines painted with sugary scenes from the life of the mother of Christ: the house of her cousin Elizabeth, the stable in Bethlehem, the carpenter's shop in

Nazareth, the house, Mount Calvary. . . . There were images of the Virgin in many house windows and shop windows in the center of town, the streets were spread with runners and carpets; anything that would serve was used as a flag or drapery hung across the streets or on the walls; every street had its own triumphal arch.

Liza, too, walked in the procession, in a prissy two-piece suit, a prissy hat on her head, a prissy handbag on her arm, a rosary in her hand. Schoolteacher. She walked devoutly beside her class of impeccably turned out ten and eleven year old boys, all of them with rosaries in their hands. Mirror of Righteousness. Seat of Wisdom. Source of our Joy. Ark of the Covenant. . . .

An hour and a half ago she had been the happy, frisking lamb and I the big bad wolf. Crawling on the deep-pile carpet on her elbows and knees she was grazing innocently, snap snap, bleat bleat, when the terrible beast leapt forth, striking his teeth into her neck and his nails into her sides, and entering her cruelly where she had already expected it, she was moist and soft there, she suffered it with her head in her hands. Gate of Heaven, Morning Star, Healer of the sick, Refuge of sinners, Comforter of the afflicted. . . . Pray for us.

Praying makes you feel peaceful.

I was standing, still naked after the game of the lamb and the wolf, behind the net curtain in the window of Liza's apartment overlooking a large square, where the procession was making its way past the houses opposite in the white afternoon light. My eyes zoomed in on Liza.

Exactly at the spot we had agreed on beforehand, she raised her hand in what looked like a flutter, and arranged something on her hat, looking at the window of her apartment where she knew I was standing behind the curtains, as a sign that she was thinking of me. But as she did so I already no longer *felt* anything for her, after I had watched her for some time moving along with the column of little boys from bead to bead and then beating time in the middle of the square while the little boys sang a song: Ma-ha-ry, my mo-ho-ther, we sing in praise of thee-hee-hee. . . .

Winding curls in the hair on my belly with my right forefinger, I thought: that Liza needed to be punished. There in that square, watched by her pupils, she would have to have her hair shorn and be stripped of her hypocritical Catholic garments; she would have to be kicked between the legs, by me, and lashed with a whip of rosaries. I would wear my blood-red frogmask. Everything I said would have to be dubbed in afterwards. Her groans and screams for mercy would be drowned by the laughter of the boys in her class.

At the same time I was one of the little boys in Liza's class; maybe Miss Liza had taught me to read and to say the Hail Mary. I would like to, brum brum, fly to her with outspread arms. To crawl inside her and disappear in her altogether, out of fear, out of

71

love, so that I would never have to be parted from her, say farewell, waving, laughing bravely although my head was filled with thundering, crashing water.

The whole world was full of mothers, but where was mine?

On the inside of the window a fly began to walk through the procession. And as if I were suddenly a different little boy, younger, smaller, knowing at once what to do, very skilled in catching small flying and creeping creatures, I trapped the fly with one hand by throwing the net curtain over it against the glass while at the same time I squashed it with the thumb of the other hand.

"Tets!" I said.

In the net curtain there was a black-red stain that was reflected in the window. By bringing my face close to the stain and then focusing my eyes in a certain way, I could see Liza's back below me in the distance, looking as if it was covered with a sheet of blood. She *must* feel that I was looking at her, at her back, her behind, the hollow of her knees, her calves. Maybe she even felt as I did:

At the moment when I pressed the fly through the meshes of the net curtain, a brief, sweet-stabbing pain shot through the area of skin between my scrotum and my anus, as if I had received in that place a thrust from a velvet-covered bayonet.

Give me understanding, give me peace.

I began to strike myself in the face, I made up my mind to do what in fact I did do when Liza returned.

She had to let herself be undressed by me with soft

fingers and then she had to lie down on the bed, on her stomach, and relax, and slumber.

I kept the flies away from her and tenderly and thoughtfully kissed and massaged and stroked her back, her buttocks and her legs, for a long long time, after having refreshed her with a little cloth with water and scent. The patch of skin I find so endearing between her vagina and her anus. That area of skin tends to tear or has to be cut when the baby's head forces its way out of the mother's body. The tear is then sewn up by a doctor with a curved needle.

Out of remorse for my lack of feeling I stroked Liza and I did not tell her that she really ought to have been raped by me as cruelly and carelessly as possible on her own dining table or kitchen work top.

Years later, I would remember all this vividly, after having forgotten it completely. I would be amazed and ashamed at it in years to come. I was like the wind, for a moment touching Liza and playfully lifting her skirts, and then going on my way again, searching.

(Why do you wear that little bell on your leg?

So as not to get lost. If I get lost in the maze, other people, for instance you, can tell where I am by that little bell.)

Have I found what I was searching for in the meantime?

Anxiety dream:

I am in bed with Liza. Her honey-colored hair hangs like a curtain in front of her face and the water pours from her body as she rides me. Laughing, she calls out invocations from the litany of the Holy Virgin. I lie on my back, smiling and lazy, my hands under my head. I let her go on, let her do as she pleases, I don't mind, we are both half drunk again, I look at her breasts, I look at the silver droplets in the hair on her belly. When she has come she lifts herself up from my member on which she had transfixed herself and she will now, kneeling between my legs, begin to cherish that member with her mouth, with her tongue, with her hands, with caresses of her soft hair, with sweet words, with crooning incantations, with oh—

But suddenly she is wearing a hat and that hair in front of her face is a veil which she arranges with both hands on the brim of her hat. The face that looks out from behind the veil is not Liza's. It is white as death itself and this death is an old woman whose hair, like cobwebs rolled into ringlets, clings to her skull—she has no breasts.

When this dead woman, who smiles at me revoltingly in a friendly, not to say motherly way, brings her tongue towards my organ, my body turns out to be all callus; it is covered with an armor of horny lumps and excrescences, I am without feeling, I am immovably heavy.

Behind my eyes there is a fluttering of mosquito nets and other gauzey tissues covered with blood stains.

Look-who-goes-there. See me marching through the mist.

Then I dream that I wake up. I am in a different room, not Liza's; there are sheets draped over all the furniture. A voice, that of a person I cannot see, which sounds as if I hear it buzzing through a telephone, asks me about each piece of furniture, whether I am interested in it. Do you want this couch? Do you want this carpet? Do you want this television set? Do you want the portrait on top of the television set?

I start to cry as I have not cried for years. The tears burst from various orifices of my body, in different ways: they spurt, splatter, ripple, dribble. The calluses on my face become soft, and then liquid, and begin to drip away from me.

I am in a maze of stage scenery, the pieces totter, in everything around me web-like cracks appear, in the mirror, for example, or the plate-glass window in front of which I am suddenly standing and which reflects my body but not my face: in my pubic hair hangs the corpse of a fly. My hands tremble so violently that I am unable to grasp or hang on to anything. And yet I try to break my rigid, callused organ in two with my fist or break it away from my body.

I see myself standing for long minutes by a pond in the woods. The clocks tick, the clocks tick. Deep in my head, I see snatches of film.

As in the garden, after the wind dies down, everything that was touched by the wind still moves for
some time, so everything I had seen at Tjideng would
move in me for three or four decades, only to be put
at rest by this: What I have written I need no longer
remember. It may now move in the conscious and
subconscious thoughts of others.

"Nothing exists that does not touch something
else."

Of that camp at Tjideng I remember especially:

The "kumpulans" or roll-calls that were held several times a day, in a square in the scorching sun, roll-
calls that everyone in the camp had to attend, infants,
the old, the healthy—insofar as anyone there was still
healthy—and those at the point of death.

All the women and children lined up in ranks, to be
counted by the Jap, and to be counted again, and to be
counted yet again, but invariably the number of prisoners did not tally with the records of the camp
administration, so that roll-calls could take hours.

When orders were shouted in Japanese everyone
had to stand motionless at attention, had to bow, had
to stand for long periods in this bowing position, had

to kneel, had to "frog-hop," had to call out together
(in Japanese): Long live the emperor!

The Jap passed in front or he passed behind or he
passed through the ranks, sowing fear and anguish
wherever he went.

"The Jap"—this term stood for: short, squat, often
puffily over-fed little men in bulging uniforms, with
faces like those of Japanese dogs or Japanese monkeys
but above all like Japanese frogs whose penetrating
eyes, set by nature in a perpetual glare or leer, pierced
you to the marrow. "The Jap": always with fixed
bayonet, rifle always at the ready, always the sun on
the steel of the bayonet, so blindingly that it seemed
to me that not only could I see the sparks of light in
the steel, but I could hear them as well: those bayonets
blared. Often "the Jap" was roaring drunk and tottered
on his plump legs as he brandished a sabre, or he held
a pistol in his hand with which, to the beat of an
unintelligible, ranted song from his fatherland, he
fired a shot into the air from time to time. There was
also a mentally disturbed Jap walking about the camp,
armed with a rattan cane stick with which he hit
everyone who crossed his path; the stick would make
a short swishing sound through the air, like a sigh,
before striking a back or a head; this Jap, have mercy
on us, always grunted like a tormented, maddened
animal. (I was good at imitating this Jap, both his
grunting and the way he moved, with little steps,
clutching the stick under his arm. I was also good at

77

reproducing the sound his weapon made when it cleaved the air before hitting someone. To make my imitation as naturalistic as possible I would squint at the same time, and sometimes I touched the tip of my nose with the tip of my tongue. So we did in fact laugh quite a bit.)

If no orders were given at roll call, there had to be absolute silence in the square, in which the only permissible sound was the stamping of the soldiers' boots. If a small child started crying, the mother would get a thrashing, if you moved you got a thrashing, if you slapped at an insect on your cheek you got a thrashing. People fainted, people collapsed from exhaustion, people fell to the ground for other reasons; on all the occasions the Jap would kick or beat them upright again, unless they were dead. People vomited from fright, or from fear, or need. They would pass water where they stood or excrete their body surpluses in some other manner. Whatever left the body was liquid, thin, yellow or light green or light red, and anyone who splattered in that way got a thrashing. Among the things that were self-evident in my early years was the notion that women had to be thrashed, or tortured or punished in other ways. After the camp, I was a grizzled adult, almost six-year-old little boy, "run wild," "immoral," "devoid of feeling." Only much later was I finally dubbed.

I never got a thrashing there. I stood firmly at attention as soon as the order "Kiotske!" was given, chest forward, shoulders back. At the order 'Kireii!' I made a deep bow. At 'Nauree!' I stood upright again. I stood under my wide hat. My shadow was the oval of my hat; according to the position of the sun it had stumps of legs, sometimes also wings when I stretched out my arms; the hat sheltered me as in later life I felt sheltered by the roof of my car, on the way here, on the way there, as if the car roof was still the hat of my childhood years.

If that square still exists, and if it is still paved with the same asphalt, perhaps the prints of my soles and toes can still be seen. Often it was so hot that the asphalt began to melt and my bare feet left sunken marks in it—so I could prove to myself that I was not made only of shadow. My soles are callused to this day, and I have no feeling in them.

"Indonesian camp children," now past forty, can be recognized by the soles of their feet, just as Dutch children, conceived and born in the "hunger winter" and now approaching forty, can still be recognized by their unbridled voracity.

For my grandmother these roll calls were the worst thing. Suffering from all the illnesses and ailments that were rife in the camp, she was finally unable to walk or stand. She had to be carried to the roll-call square and afterwards to be carried back to her place in the kitchen cabinet. For a time my mother carried my grandmother on her back. One day, however, she devised a vehicle that was soon named the "goat cart," later shortened to "the goat."

Somehow my mother had got hold of an ironing board and somehow she had managed to get a pair of roller skates.

How did one acquire such things in the camp? By bartering other possessions, preferably food: a bra for a handful of sugar, a shawl for a needle, a handbag for an ironing board.

At the front end and back end of the ironing board my mother fixed a roller skate, so that the board rested on wheels. My grandmother was stretched out on the ironing board, with a cloth over her face to protect her from the sun, the flies and the shame; my sister and I had to steady the cart on either side to stop it from tilting, and my mother pulled it along by a string, like a goat.

How we laughed!

Of those trips I remember that my grandmother, "to keep up her spirits," would crack odd kinds of jokes that often had to do with "language" and that confused me and have continued to intrigue me to the present day. She would say things like: "There goes Kate with a bun on her . . . saucer." Or: "I am Jack Hall, I put my stick, against the . . . fence." Or she would ask: "Is it true that a gnu says moo when he's done . . . nothing?"

How we laughed!

Remembered till the present day and finally written down, with the intention to leave it and not to cross it out again—in anticipation of the moment at which, perhaps, the unriddling of all things will take place.

During roll call we supported grandmother on all sides to keep her standing up. I remember that she leaned on me and it was as though she was not leaning on me. She remained standing until the very end, but then it really was the very end.

She admonished us always, in moments of utter despair, to think of "something else," it did not matter what, because whatever we thought of would be less terrible than the things we saw, "as if you could switch on a machine and then see things you liked to see."

Ten years later it would be called television.

Of "despair" I still had no notion then, nor did I ever succeed later in thinking of "something else" other than what I saw and witnessed. I have no imagination.

If now I think back on those camp years, of the way I experienced them in one way or another, my first association is a picture accompanied by the sound of fluttering flags. Around the camp, every so many meters, there was a watch tower in which a Jap with binoculars and a machine gun surveyed the camp from above, and a flag flew on each of these towers. In my memory the camp was encircled by at least a hundred flags. These flags were white, and in the center, completely surrounded by white, was a red ball: the symbol of the sun, the symbol of the rising sun. In terms of graphic design the Japanese flag is the most beautiful of all national flags (I thought so even then). But it was impressed upon me that I must not see the Japanese flag in it but, whenever I saw it, I must "pretend" it was the Dutch tricolor: red–white–blue.

"But I can't see any blue."

"The sky in which that flag flies is blue."

"Pretending" that something is not what it is but "something else"—maybe people who can do that are "happy," calm and free of anxiety.

It's hard to attain a place in the sun. Once attained the sun is extinguished.

I think I would be a bad writer if I was "happy": happy writers have nothing to say.

Why should I have thought of "something else" or "pretended" that I did not see what was going on, when during one of those roll calls something happened that would be the end for my grandmother?

On that occasion the camp commandant appeared at the roll call, Mister Kenichi Sone in person, seated on a horse. It was not the first time I had seen him, but it was the first time I saw a horse. Sone was decked out in stars and breast plates that reflected the sun, he wore a sword by his side. His upper body swaying, he floated past in the heat vapor that rose from the asphalt. As I remember it he must have been roughly as old as I am now. I don't suppose he noticed me.

Watch it, there is always someone in the crowd who remembers you. Perhaps that little boy is the writer who, almost forty years later, will write that he has seen you rocking by, standing out against the clouds, sprinkled with sparks of sunlight, the son of the sun who would later be executed as a criminal, the vicar of god himself, whom the pope had kissed lovingly on the cheeks: *pax tibi.*

Whenever Sone appeared, something terrible had happened outside the camp for which the inmates were to be punished: the Japanese fleet had suffered losses, the advance of the allies had begun in Europe, with a newfangled bomb the Americans had blown away a Japanese city from the face of the earth.

Erect in the saddle, Sone made a speech that his horse understood at least: sometimes the animal nodded or stamped a spark out of the ground with his hoof by way of assent—how handy that a horse has a long tail with which it can whisk the flies from his body.

To conclude his speech, the commandant called out: "Tenno-heika banzai!" (Hurrah for the emperor!), which the prisoners, forced to their knees and with their faces against the ground, had to repeat many times at the top of their voices. Banzai!

Then, for the thousands of women and children, the "frog-hopping" began. Squatting on all fours you had to leap like a frog until you heard the blood roaring in your head like a storm and you felt your heart thumping in your throat, and at the back of your knees and in other parts of your body, as if it was trying to leap out of you. The sun, meanwhile, did not shine any more gently and time did not pass any more quickly. Who can describe the length of a moment, who can describe the duration of the fifteen, twenty minutes that one is forced to hop on one's haunches in a bell jar of murderous heat?

Everywhere bayonets flashed, everywhere the Jap ranted, shouting who knows what in his terrifying oracle tongue, everywhere bodies were falling, dragging other bodies with them, and in the swirl of bodies there arose an undercurrent of scrambling and crawling at which the Jap hit out with rifle butts, sticks, whips. Mother most pure, Mother most admirable, Mother most wonderful, Mother most amiable.

At every hop I made, my hat bounced and I felt it fall back on my head with a plop, as if I were being tapped on the skull by a finger, by someone reminding me that I must keep looking at what I saw and not pretend to see something different, because one day I would have to write it down—it was part of the predestination of all things.

That time, dozens of women did not survive the frog hopping. There were some who lay down in exhaustion and did not want to get up again, not even after the Jap had danced on them. There were some who went crazy and started attacking the Jap, they were hooked by a bayonet or shot down.

The Jap now decreed that at every frog-hop we had to call out "croak croak!" I knew better than to laugh at that.

84

Sone, on his horse, swayed among the hopping and croaking bodies. Perhaps he was grinning, perhaps not. Perhaps he was filled with vicious, sadistic pleasure, perhaps not. Perhaps he had had an experience in his early years that had determined his whole future life, so that he was incurably tainted with contempt, lovelessness and insensitivity towards women, just as I would be. I am one who does not know what love is, who is unable to "feel" anything in connection with that word. In that respect, perhaps, I am just like camp commandant Kenichi Sone. Women: croak croak! Hear our prayer, O Lord, and have mercy upon us. Some women, as a result of the inhuman hopping with its continuous jerking on the organs inside their abdomen, began to turn themselves inside out. Together with their excreta, the dislodged organs left their bodies; as they hopped they gave birth to blood and slime.

I am one who is not moved by "the miracle of birth," I am one who stays home when his child is born in the hospital.

(Most important, the other day the birth of my daughter kept me from my work: the study I was writing on suicide in Dutch literature. Do not disturb! Leave me in peace! "Motherhood" and "motherliness"—these things do not fit into my life.

I did not want to see my beloved wife, whom I adored for her beauty, splitting or being split by scissors. The cobblestone that would appear and protrude from her body, a cobblestone that could never be pushed back into that same hole. All those wails of agony and screams of pain, all that blood, all that slush, but most of all the outrageous sight of the destruction of or at least the lasting injury to beauty, and *my* disgust at it, *my* remorse at it, *my* helplessness, *my* protest, *my* fear and *my* vicarious longing, which is: the longing felt by me on behalf of the child wrenched forth, not to be doomed to live but to be allowed to return at once through that hole-in-time from which my own head once emerged.

As soon as I heard by phone that my daughter was born, I drove to the hospital where, entering the white sun-drenched labor ward, I found that I was there and at the same time somewhere else. True, I was forty, balding and greying, but I was also a little boy, surrounded by quacking, and forced to look at what I saw without pretending to see something else. I was back at Tjideng and it was as if one of my feet was heavier than the other and I would be rooted to the ground with that one foot.

On the table a naked woman lay on her back, her legs up and spread out. In front of the table, on a stool, sat a doctor, busy refashioning the ravages between the woman's legs. All that had been torn open there and would never arouse my tenderness again, since it had been damaged for good, he was sewing up with needle and thread—the needle he used was sickle-shaped. The ravages: a fleece of blood clung to her inner thighs; from the wide, gaping chasm between them, blood and other blood-red liquid rippled out. It dripped audibly, like raindrops, from the edge of the table into a white bowl between the doctor's feet on the floor of the ward. So much blood! It was as though a gunshot had been fired at the central point of this woman's body.

All those mothers, so many mothers.

It occurred to me that I had once thought, now I want a different mother.

The sleeping child in the metal crib beside the table on which the woman lay was my daughter. I gave her—nothing exists or has existed that does not cause, has not caused or will not cause something else—the name that is the only name she can bear, all her life, all the rest of my life.

Then I drove home in my car, the roof of which sheltered me like a wide hat, in order to resume, supposedly untouched, unaffected, unperturbed, the work I had interrupted. But my hands trembled so violently that I was unable to write and the pen kept falling from my fingers.)

In the roll call square full of croaking frog-women and frog-children, my grandmother was being helped in her frog-hopping by my mother and another woman and at a certain moment I saw her topple over. I heard the sigh that escaped her, sounding, amidst the croaking of the thousands of mouths around us, as if she were singing. Her face was so covered with sweat that it looked as if she were wearing a liquid mask that fell from her in trickles and dribbles.

In my memory the most terrible detail is this:

When my grandmother's head hit the ground, her bun came undone and her hair fell in thin grey strands beside her cheeks. I, who had never seen my grandmother other than with that bun, must have realized that with its undoing the decomposition of her body had begun. I knew she was dying now and that the flies would soon settle on her without being brushed away by her or anyone else.

My mother and the other woman began to tug at my grandmother, to get her upright again, in whatever position. They did this still frog-hopping and croaking. My grandmother managed to rise to her knees and then sank back, her behind on her heels; her spectacles, held together with sticking plaster, string and bits of wire, now seemed broken for good. Blood poured out of her nose and mouth and fell among the flowers on her dress. She could frog-hop no more, she let herself fall forward and, leaning on her elbows, her head in her hands, she began to make helpless, rocking movements from side to side, pray for us sinners, now and in the hour of our death.

It occurred to me that someone ought to comb my grandmother's hair, or at least see to it that it did not trail through the blood in those wisps (which reminded me of paint brushes, dipped in red, painting Japanese characters on the asphalt). It occured to me that we ought to say thousands of Hail Marys, and also that it would be of no use, no use at all.

Although I tried hard to imagine a little gadget that

could be switched on so that one could see scenes that were pleasanter than the scenes one saw in reality, I succeeded less than ever. I did not want to see something different from what I saw or think of something different from what I saw. I wanted to see *nothing* and think of *nothing*. I did not want to be anywhere, I did not want to exist. I would not have minded dying together with my grandmother or even instead of my grandmother, while the last thing I would see, the last thing that would settle on my retina, would be a color: red, the color of death, which sat like a splash of blood on the Japanese flag.

Hopping on my heels and croaking harder than anyone, in order to smother everything that welled up in me with the sound of my own voice and to drown all the sounds around me in the sound of my own voice, I turned away from my grandmother and my mother and began, hand on my hat, to hop among the other frog-bodies, croak-croak-croak, Danny— in search, on the way to non-being, but really I was in search of Nettie Stenvert. I wanted to tell her something but I could not remember what.

I found her, hopping hand in hand with her mother who had lost her head scarf and was now, with shorn head like so many women, at the mercy of the sun. With little hops I maneuvered myself into a position behind Nettie, so I could look at her dark blonde ringlets that danced so merrily at every hop she made and then fell back against her cheeks and on her neck in such a way that for a moment I could not croak because I had to swallow. Kiss me and I shall change into a prince.

In that one moment in which I was silent I heard the thousand-throated frog-call around me, mingled with all the other things that could be heard: shots, blows, curses, weeping, the clatter of hooves, the stamping of boots, and for the first time in my life I was seized by the panic that has to do with death, dying, being dead, wanting to be dead (but I was certain that I would not die until all the others, even Kenichi Sone, even Kenichi Sone's horse, yes perhaps even Nettie, had died, for I would first have to bear witness to my life, that is *life* in the span of time during which I was to live).

With a leap I landed beside Nettie, and even before she had looked around to see who was suddenly croaking at the top of his voice, I saw that her face too was wet; sweat ran from her forehead and eyebrows into her eyes where I saw it glistening like silver paper. It made me think of the eyes of her doll, the way she blinked to squeeze the wet out of them.

Panting, I told her, "Our grandma is going to die." That is what I said, while it flashed through my mind that I had really wanted to tell her something else— something very festive and, in connection with it, something that filled me with pride and gladness, but I could not remember what it was.

"Then I'll tchoop that bead-thing of your grandma's that she is always mumbling prayers over," said Nettie, also panting.

"It's called a rosary," I croaked. "If you're not a Catholic and you touch a rosary the beads will burn holes in your hands."

Nettie was not shocked at this, any more than I would have been shocked at it. We actually experienced things that were just as terrible—and the most terrible was this: that in the end we could no longer be shocked, could no longer be moved, were no longer capable of feeling anything. We had become like the callused soles of our feet.

Perhaps this explains the laughter of those who lived through the Japanese camps more consciously than I, and survived them: better to "pretend" that "something different" happened than that which actually did happen; better to laugh than to live through it once again in your mind, better not to think about it any more at all.

This event, which made frogs of us all, took place on April 30, 1945. That day was my fifth birthday. My mother gave me a book with which she could complete the reading lessons she had given me and which I was soon able to read for myself, *Danny goes on a trip*. Who knows which of her paltry possessions my mother had to barter away in order to acquire that book. It was a smudged, damaged copy, some of the pages were loose, some were even missing, but I was proud and happy, as I would be again some twenty years later when I held in my hands the first book I, myself, had written.

In April 1945 the Japanese island of Okinawa was

captured and the decisive air offensive against Japan began. On my birthday that year, Adolf Hitler committed suicide in the flattened city of Berlin, by shooting himself in the mouth with a revolver. The prisoners at Tjideng were most gruesomely punished for these events.

My grandmother died four days later, on her shelf in the kitchen cabinet.

We saw and heard her body decompose into bubur while she was still alive, and the beads of her rosary slipped ever more slowly through her fingers. First her thin body began to swell and was covered with large brown patches, then she began to ooze, then the cabinet became filled with an indescribable and unbearable stench, so that my sister and I would not sleep in it any more, on the floor below my grandmother.

On the 4th of May my mother, wailing loudly the way she had wailed when she was beaten, wrapped her mother in a rush mat and lifted the limp bundle onto the ironing board. While she pulled the ironing board along by a string, and my sister and I steadied the cart on either side, we trundled our grandmother through the streets for the last time and handed her over at the gate house.

She lies buried somewhere in present-day Jakarta, in a cemetery full of identical white wooden crosses: grave number 74.

She was a gentle, patient, and, they say, very witty woman.

After these last rites my sister and I scooted home cheering and shouting, each on one roller skate. My mother carried the ironing board because it might still serve as something for barter, and from that time on my grandmother's rosary hung like a chain around my mother's neck.

In June 1945 my sister tumbled head first into the open sewer in front of the house we lived in. She disappeared in the camp hospital—dysentery—and as she seemed to disappear more and more, like my grandmother, my mother laughed less and less, and when she did laugh she did so more briefly, and no longer showing her teeth.

The only thing I was concerned about was the loss of the roller skate that was not fished up from the sewer along with my sister.

On the 29th of July 1945, we heard later, my grandfather, the composer, died.

On a day in the first half of August 1945, Nettie Stenvert died.

On the 2nd of September 1945 Japan capitulated. Even after that we stayed in the camp for several more months.

The device you can switch on to see scenes you want to see, less terrible than the things you would otherwise see, or than the things which overpower your soul and of which you cannot think without fear and trembling.

In the last few hours of my mother's life, Dutch television offered the following programs:

Netherlands 1, at 7:00 P.M.: "The K.R.O. drops in . . . in Dordrecht." "Variety program from the Merwede Hall. Assisted by Tommy Reilly, Ted de Braak, Thérèse Steinmetz, Joke Bruys, the Vienna Bears, Bloem, Aunt Leen, Joe Harris, Los Allegros, the International Folklore Dance Theatre. Presented by Hans van Willigenburg."

It is likely that if my mother had her television switched on she had seen this program flickering before her, not the pop-music program "Star Club," which was shown at the same time on Netherlands 2. The chance for relaxation was greater on Netherlands 1. She needed to relax.

At 7:55 the program "In the first row for a postcard" began. Bob Bouma's film magazine. Special guest Rijk de Gooyer, speaking about his role in the new Dutch feature film, *Forbidden Bacchanal,* directed by Wim Verstappen.

At that moment my mother probably switched to Netherlands 2: The Ster:

"Hello there, how are you? Tomorrow at Peek & Cloppenburg's." "The secret you share with Sandeman." "Victoria Vesta insures the modern way. Victoria Vesta feels safe." "Pankie is always a treat. Glorious Pankie. From Victoria." "Silan Supersoft, Reaches deepest into the skin."

Dong, 8:00 P.M. The News.

The fifty-two American hostages who were imprisoned for four hundred and forty-four days in Iran, have arrived in the United States. The widow of Mao Tse Tung, Jiang Qing, has been sentenced to death by a special court in Peking. Stay of execution will be granted. Igloo, the frozen food company, has been selling tainted products. For the third time, the Liberal Party has selected Mr. Hans Wiegel to top its list in the coming elections. In the Slangenburg district in Gelderland, forty members of the Mobile Unit and one hundred uniformed policemen were brought into action today to close down the illegal radio station Radio Milano. The weather: mostly dry with some chance of fog. Temperature: from 2 to 6 degrees.

Then The Ster again:

"We had it just yesterday. My own home-made soup." "Fa Deodorant with the natural freshness of lemons." "For the small in-between wash. Hip hip, hurray!" "Since that's what he likes, Mister Mikes."

After that, on Netherlands 2, *Deadly Knowledge,* exciting British serial, part 2 ("Kirby is still not sure whether Laura is an agent or an unknowing accomplice in the affair. She certainly has spoken about him to her stepfather Fane. Kirby is sent to France, to get hold of a coded message that has been left there. An interview with one Madame Lafois proves necessary. Kirby: John Gregson. Laura: Prunella Ransome. Madame Lafois: Elisabeth Bergner").

My mother would not have watched this program, nor did she watch *Gunsmoke* (American Western serial. This episode: *The Widowmaker,* which started at 8:40 on Netherlands 1).

Around that time she phoned my sister. She was unhappy and frightened, she cried. She had called to thank my sister for two letters that she had not answered because she trembled so that she could not keep the pen in her hand, let alone write with it. And she wanted to tell my sister that she thought about the conversation they had had at Christmas all the time, but that she couldn't do anything about it now, it was too late, she couldn't stop crying, she felt so tense, as if something was going to happen.

Had she taken her pills yet, my sister asked. No, she hadn't. Well, do that first.

The pills my mother took to quiet her anxieties and to allay the trembling of her hands and head are called Eldopal Retard, Sinemet, Disipal (all of them for Parkinson's disease), Pyridoxine Labaz (for all sorts of degenerative disease), Librium (for all sorts of things that have names and all sorts of things that are nameless), Glifanan (for pain), Calcium Sandoz (for fatigue), Mogadon (in order to sleep and to counteract the side effects of all the other drugs she swallowed). How poetic these names are, as poetic as rose, phlox, convolvulus—flowers in my garden that move when the wind touches them. It was too late. It was too late.

Then my sister asked if she had eaten anything. No, she hadn't. My mother wasn't hungry. You must eat something, my sister said. Fix yourself a sandwich. And then do try to go to sleep.

At 9:20 my mother, because she loved to laugh, may have watched "Are you being served?"—popular British sitcom, on Netherlands 2. ("This episode: Everything for insurance. Grace Brothers Department Store organizes a medical check-up for its personnel, for insurance purposes. Everyone prepares for a thorough examination. Mr. Humphries: John Inman. Mrs. Slocombe: Mollie Sugden).

That program ended at 9:50, and the news program "TV Topics of the Day" began. My mother would have turned off the set to get ready for bed; perhaps everything would be all right tomorrow. She looked at her husband's portrait on the television set, she moved it half an inch as she always did when she was near it, perhaps she fleetingly thought of phoning someone else, perhaps even me, and perhaps her wish and her longing that the phone would suddenly ring in her apartment were so strong that she *expected* it to ring, and had already stretched out her trembling hand toward the receiver.

The last scenes that unfolded before her she did not see on the television screen. They must have been scenes from the film of her own life, many of which she had forgotten. She saw again the faces of all the people in her life; she was back in all the places, in all the houses, in all the rooms in which her life had been enacted. (She had been so brave all her life. Her indestructible optimism, her never-failing cheerfulness.)

One of the scenes must have been of the time she lay asleep on top of the kitchen cabinet at Tjideng, with me sitting beside her in my jumpsuit of red, blue, red–blue and purple dots, my feet covered with calluses, making myself very small so as not to disturb her. I am the last thing she has left, as she is the last thing I have left. With my hat I fan coolness at her, looking sharp that no flies settle on her; it is clear that I do not want my mother to die, if my mother dies I will read softly to her from my books.

This same scene I myself shall see before long in the film of my own life, and I shall see in that film that, decades later, I put this scene into words in some book or other that I am writing—a writer like me lives his life twice: the second time when he puts into words what he has experienced the first time.

So my mother had finally come to the point where she lived from hour to hour, and then from minute to minute and then from second to second. With the taste of cheese in her mouth she finally saw herself falling from a couch onto a carpet, and she began her long staring into the flames of the fireplace that made her calm—calmer than she had ever been in her life.

"Prosper and be happy wherever you may go."

Death is a monumental blood-red frog. He sits greedily on the bank of a wide river which is the river of souls. Like a harpoon he hurls out his tongue, his jaws grind unhurriedly, there is a rustling between them before he swallows. Then he aims his harpoon afresh. Where he sits there is the quackng of countless dubbed languages, uttered by his servants. Where he sits there is no longer any sunrise, the sun is everlastingly red in the center of some universe or other, everlastingly wrapped in mist.

The clocks tick.

My mother died, and at about the same time I showed my guest out, saying to him, leave me in peace, I won't join any union, I don't want to join anything, I'll do everything on my own, I am all calluses from top to bottom. (Translated, it means: I am afraid, I am sick with hatred, it is too late for me to cure myself.)

My mother died and at about the same time I thought of Liza. In my imagination she was standing by the window in the town where she lives, restless, thinking of me as I thought of her, she was standing by the phone which might ring any moment now, she had a feeling as if someone were blowing at her.

I saw this forgotten film scene:

Me, years ago, the morning after the procession, after I had left Liza, and was already behind the wheel of my car, while she stood, in her delicate transparent dragonfly-colored nightgown, at the window of her apartment. With one hand she held the curtain back, with the other she waved to me and I waved back, languidly, having gratified myself, carelessly, once more in her body while thinking: when this is over I shall get away at last. Virgin most prudent. Virgin most venerable. Virgin most renowned.

At the moment I started my car the door of the clock shop under Liza's window opened. The shopkeeper came out onto the sidewalk. In one hand he held a long pole with a hook at the end, in the other he held a bunch of keys. He stuck the hook into the ring underneath the metal roller blind which had been lowered over his shop window and which consisted of a lattice-work of bars. He pushed one of the keys into the lock that fastened the blind, and fumbled jerkily in the keyhole for some time. The lattice began to rattle upwards, hampered in its ascent by the hook at the end of the pole that the shopkeeper held in both hands and let slip slowly. I saw clocks appear in the window. Indus, Prisma, Pontiac, Zenith, Longines, Certina. It was about half-past eight. Amid the dozens of clocks stood a statue of the virgin, in white porcelain, between two vases of withered flowers.

Me, at the wheel, hand on the gear shift which I had put in reverse, right foot pressing hard on the gas pedal, the bell on my trousers tinkling—that was the stage scene in which I saw Liza, who stood by the window as if on a television screen, slowly receding. Under the chain of beads that represented a rosary I drove out of the town, past the stable in Bethlehem, the house in Nazareth, and all the other places of the life of the mother of Christ.

The last thing I saw before I drove away from the square where Liza looked out, waving goodbye, bye, bye-bye, was:

that just below the window sill behind which she stood the lattice rolled up all by itself and that at the level of the invisible (as if painted in gold, sacred) intersection of Liza's thighs, the hook at the end of the pole was lifted out of the ring of the roller blind, and it was as though, for a split second, I saw this soon-to-be-forgotten beloved in her gauzy garment impaled on the tip of the pole.

The phone rang. It was the home where my mother had died.

The voice that a few days before had informed me of my mother's death now asked me if I wanted any furniture or other objects from among my mother's possessions: the management of the home wanted to let her apartment without delay, from the first of the month. They had started emptying the apartment before my mother had been taken to the crematorium.

Let us pray.

Did I want her as-good-as-new and completely-paid-for color television set? Did I want her couch, her carpet, this Chinese vase, that painting of a pale blue mountain in Java with yellow rice paddies in the foreground, her bedspread, her wadyan, her rosary, her crossword-puzzle dictionary of one million words?

I wanted nothing—I did not want to "tchoop" anything (except maybe her eyeglasses, but I did not tell them that).

Weeks later I received the iconography of my mother's life: all her photo albums, in which I looked, for days on end, at all the places, all the houses, all the rooms where her life had been enacted, in which I studied the faces of all the people in her life, her parents, her brother, her sister, her husband, her husband's parents, brothers and sister, her children, her children-in-law, her grandchildren, her friends, her acquaintances, housemates.

But where was she herself?

I appear in my mother's photo albums less than anyone else; at some point I vanished from her life and she vanished from mine.

Together with the photo albums I came into possession of my father's portrait which had watched my mother for seventeen years from the top of her television set, and it is as if I am the one that watched her from that place; it is that face I see when I look in the mirror—balding skull, grey-white hair, roughly at the end of the second act of my life, just before the intermission.

I thought: I am an orphan almost forty-one years old. From a literary point of view it is trash, and as psychology it is worthless, but I thought it all the same.

What was to be done with all those—more than a thousand—photographs? (Everything is draped in white sheets and these are covered with cobwebs, the people who used to live here are all dead.) Better to let it all be blown away by the wind.

Passages of a letter from my mother to her husband, written at Batavia C while she was still in the camp at Tjideng, on October 5, 1945:

"My dearest Sjoekie, How happy I was to get your letter this morning. At last a sign of life after nearly two years. Your last letter from Tokyo was dated 8 December '43; after that nothing more; you can imagine how I longed for news from you, and especially when you see letters arriving all around you every day, and men coming home, well then it gets a bit too much at times. Though I prayed with the little ones to Our Lady every day for Daddy's safe return, and now our prayer has been answered. We may be thankful indeed that we are all together, safe and sound, and ready to start a new life with fresh courage, if necessary starting from scratch if we must, but all of us together. I am glad you really are well and that you have gained weight. How thin you must have been at 47 kilos. Have there been no nasty after effects—I have often thought of your eyes, because I heard of blindness so often. Well, next time I hope you'll write in more detail. And now you are in Manila. I have shown the boys exactly where that is on the map. How much longer Sjoekie? You have been gone almost four years now, you don't know how terribly I long for you. . . .

"I am all right at the moment. I weighed only 38 kilos and looked more like a skeleton than anything else—puffy legs, blotches from lack of vitamins, well, all kinds of troubles, but now that we can get what we need again I am recovering quite well. I already weigh 42 kilos, and I am beginning to look better. I don't need to wear a brooch any more to show which side is the front. . . .

"Mother and Dad both died, quite soon, one after the other. Mother on the 4th of May this year, from dysentery, hunger, edema and total exhaustion. Dad at the end of July, I don't know the exact date yet, and I don't know the cause either, but in his case it is just as well, because he would miss Mother so much. It has hit me very hard too, especially Mother's death. . . ."

About my sister: ". . . . She is a big girl now and she is so practical. She lights the fire and cooks and so on, it's a treat to watch her, she is so funny. I think your fatherly heart would burst with pride, she is a real darling, as fairhaired as ever. . . .

"And then our Jeroen, the little rascal, none of the others was ever so naughty. He is the spitting image of you, both inside and out, a miniature you in everything, and he has been a great comfort to me through these terrible years. He takes your photograph to bed with him every night, how sweet he is. . . .

"Darling, I have had a nice long chat with you, I must stop now to catch the mail. I hope to hear from you again soon and even more to see you. Lots of love and kisses from us all, longingly, *your little wife*.

"P.S. Could you make inquiries about Pieter Franciscus Stenvert, Sergeant of the Land Reserves number 168816. He was in Sensuy."

On Friday, January 30, at 1500 hours my mother was cremated.

By choosing cremation she spared me the anguish that still assails me whenever I think of all those others who died and who were not cremated but buried: what would he look like now in his grave, in what state of decomposition would her body be now. . . . I do not have to imagine that my mother's body is decomposing into bubur; my mother has perished in the way a diamond perishes—in the hottest, most loving embrace of flames.

During the ceremony the Largo from Beethoven's Triple Concerto was played first; then the Marche Funèbre from Beethoven's piano sonata number twenty-six; then the In Paradisum from the Duruflé's Requiem: "Into paradise the angels may lead thee."

I have had the ceremony described to me in detail, minute by minute. Later I saw color photographs of it, after first having made sure that among these photographs there would not be one of my mother in her coffin; I did not want to see my mother dead, I want to remember her as she was in my life. Even though she was not present, she was at any rate alive, for she dialed my number from time to time; from time to time I heard her voice.

The coffin in which my mother lay was buried under flowers that had come "from the four quarters of the earth," the room smelled sweet and festive.

In between the music there were speeches. My mother's courage. And: "She was like a queen." "She was the most beautiful mother." An extract was read from a novel, *The Submerged,* by her son, the author: "My mother and I . . . and suddenly there appears between her and me an unfathomable abyss. . . . I see myself sinking away in it, rotating on my axis . . . she has let me go, I have fallen out of her arms. . . . Oh, where are your eyes, mother mine."

That afternoon I drove my car, alone, through the neighborhood I live in, "on the way," here, there, nowhere, longing not to be. The roof of my car shielded me like a hat that was too big for me. The windshield wipers cleared the glass of my cockpit, it was misty, an almost imperceptible moisture was descending, brum-brum, Danny the fighter pilot, Danny's mother vanishes from the earth.

Beside me—this is what I wanted—Liza should have been sitting. She would lay her calm, cool hand on me and speak perhaps one word and my soul would be healed. I trembled all over, all the way to the sole of my foot pressing on the accelerator, so that my trembling was audible and palpable even in the engine. The rustling of her clothes and the sound of her voice. That little laugh of hers. Oh come and comfort me (but I do not want to love you, nor do I want you to love me or to begin to love me). Wait, wait quietly. It will not be long now. Do you know what time of night it is? Yes, I do, I do. I want to finish one more long book, don't disturb me, as it is all this is keeping me from my work. Tabé Mamma, bye, bye-bye, you are floating away in the river of souls and I don't have my pills with me. I have no thoughts about your death, except the sort that from a literary point of view must be categorized as trash. Oh Liza, I *feel* nothing, but every night you may come to me in my dream, wave to me, with the curtain in your window; in the transparent delicate blue of your nightgown I see the golden down under your arm. Bye, bye-bye, Tabé nyonya, mater dolorosa, now you vanish, in your best dress with the cloudlike patterns, into the fire, and the plume of smoke you leave behind will dissolve in the mist. Presently, at home, I will take another "Seresta Forte," or I will get drunk on gin, to relieve my physical discomfort and to console myself for all the other things, to be gone, gone from the world, gone from myself.

Somewhere, in a place where I suddenly found myself—a place I did not recognize but that seemed familiar nonetheless, a place, it turned out later, near my home, that I had reached, misled by the mist and the confusion of my thoughts, after having driven around in circles for hours—I turned into a woodland path, unable to arrest my trembling and to control the car properly.

I began to trot through the wood as if I were being

pursued or as if I were in a hurry to get somewhere on time, crazy with fears I could not define or rationalize; there was the same fog in my head as in the wood. In the wood, fog had piled up among the bare and not-bare trees into towers, castles and gothic churches; I was in a ghostly city where everything was festooned with draperies of spider-web that looked like old, dead hair full of dried-out insects, every thread was covered with tiny raindrops, there were triumphal arches formed by the rank growth of thousands of bracket-fungi in thousands of color variations, every-thing dripping, everything apparently undiscovered and untrodden. Look who goes there. Who would dare venture without a bell into this grey labyrinth?

I did not run among these trees, the trees ran around me, stretching out their branches to my face, to rip it from me like a mask and give me a face of mist in return. I did not push my way into the wood, the wood pushed itself upon me, as if made up of stage props that had started walking of their own accord, encircling me and pushing banks of fog be-fore them in which I saw myself becoming invisible, as if I was vanishing into a hole in time:

I am five years and a few months old, I am wearing my monkey suit with colored dots, I am wearing my topi, I am wearing my shoes of calluses and on my right foot a roller skate.

It is early August 1945. I am—but I do not know it yet—at an epicenter of world history: what happens now will change the face of the earth, god is being ungodded, life itself will never be as it was before these days, for at one blow all epochs have come to an end and the end is marked by what shall be visible for centuries—the scar of a burn on the skin of the world and of all mankind.

On August 6th, an atom bomb falls on Hiroshima. Three days later an atom bomb falls on Nagasaki.

As a punishment for these bombings the inmates of Tjideng are herded into the square and have to stand at attention for twelve, thirteen hours; the Jap goes around shooting, sabering, whipping; there is to be more frog-hopping and croaking.

On this occasion the Jap tears up all the paper that can be found in the camp, bibles, prayer books, other literature, diaries, drawings, letters (but I carry my own book, *Danny goes on a trip,* next to my bare skin; among the pages of this book I keep my father's photograph in his uniform of the Royal Netherlands-

Indonesian Army), the Jap cuts mattresses open and chucks the kapok around like a burrowing dog, the Jap smashes window panes, the Jap breaks up floors, the Jap sets fire to the run-down houses in the camp, so that clothes, clogs, mosquito nets, furniture (including our ironing board) crumble to ashes.

There is not much left that can be burned or otherwise destroyed, but these are the last precious possessions of the living dead in the camp.

Who can appreciate the value of a saucepan or a can or a ladle or a chamber pot, when it is the last thing one has, in which to keep the most precious thing one can have in a concentration camp in the tropics: water, very little water, five drops, for which one has waited in line for hours, because in each street there is only one water tap, set, moreover, with deliberate spite to deliver the merest trickle of water.

Who can know how precious is the box or canister or anything else that has a lid, unless he knows that such an object has to serve as a safe for the few crumbs of bread or the few grams of rice that are sometimes issued on those rare occasions when there is something other than bubur, and that this food has to be used sparingly because no one knows if and when new rations will be issued, and one must also guard against thieving fellow inmates: people, rats and cockroaches, all of them greedy for food, all of them living only because of the instinct to stay alive.

The Jap goes about with the express purpose of destroying the whole camp, just as in Europe, which had already been liberated by this time, the Hun went about in the last days of the war completely destroying some of his concentration camps—erasing them from the landscape so that no evidence would remain, so that nothing could be proved.

We are standing in the sun, I on my roller skate leaning against my mother, clutching her thin thigh with both arms. Her body is clammy the way all camp bodies are clammy; they are bodies that can no longer sweat, because of the dirt and because there is hardly any moisture left inside them to be sweated out (or wept out—these bodies weep without losing moisture. These women's bodies no longer menstruate either, because there is not enough blood left in them).

Toward evening, when the sun, red as a chopped-off head, sinks into the earth, Commandant Sone appears in the yard. He is on foot, but he wears boots with spurs that clink at every step. He has a rattan stick with which he thrashes the air about him. The almost singing sound that this makes can be heard in the farthest corners of the square, in the most hidden convolutions of my brain, where it is stored in the sound-archives of my memory. He is drunk and stays on his feet with difficulty, his eyes are red, as are the stars, medals and all the other glinting things with which he is decked out, all red: the color of the sky is reflected in them, the color of the sky is still red after the sun has gone down: whole blocks of houses are on fire, the flames replace the heat and light of the sun

113

that I have watched setting in the decorations on Sone's chest.

The Commandant delivers a speech that goes on for hours, in the course of which he keeps threatening to fall down. Sometimes he draws his sabre, then his pistol, he is extremely angry and he feels extremely hot; his head is liquid, because he sweats so much, sheds so many tears, sprays so much spittle at every shouted word—which ought to be dubbed into some intelligible language, since none of the women and children can understand what he says.

(I do not have to understand what he says in order to understand *him*. I watch his wet face with fascination, I watch the way it drips away from him in dribbles and trickles. Does Sone have a mother too? Do Japs have mothers? Is Sone's mother dead, and is that why he is making that tremendous, dramatic speech while the stage is burning and the hundreds of extras are looking up at him with nothing in their hollow bodies but hate, their stomachs rattling like frogs?)

Banzai! Banzai! Banzai!

Picks, spades and shovels are distributed, and when Sone himself has indicated a place a few meters away from where I am standing, hat on one ear, leaning with my cheek against my mother's thigh, the women begin to open up the soft asphalt and start hacking and digging a hole, meters wide and deep, in the red earth that becomes visible underneath.

The Jap decrees that there shall be singing. The

"camp song", that must have sprung up by accident one day: "Let the bell go ringing / let the bell sound loud / there's no one in the whole wide world / that can bring Tjideng down. . . ."

Beside the hole a woman beats time, swinging both arms. Sone, who is standing beside her, beats out the rhythm of the song with his stick on her backside and her calves. His head is red, at each breath his chest swells like a frog's throat; he feeds on the blood and the bodies of flies.

I sing bravely, balancing on my one leg on the roller skate, which is fastened with broken straps and bits of string to my bare foot. I don't take my eyes off Sone, tabé tuan, in him I greet lurking Death in person.

Later I learned it had been feared, during that night, as part of the complete destruction of the camp, that all the inmates would be shot dead, ten or twenty at a time, until the freshly dug hole was full of bodies, after which other women would have had to dig another hole, using the earth to cover the first, whereupon they themselves would be shot, to fill the new hole with their bodies, and so forth. All this while singing "Hop Marjanneke," "Where are you going, my pretty maid," "High on the yellow haycart" and even, because the Jap ordered there *must* be singing, never mind what, "We won't go home until morning, we won't go home until morning. . . ."

When they tell me this, later, they do so laughingly, in a tone of what could be interpreted as affection—yes, even as nostalgia; first their hatred mellowed and then disappeared; people died the death called "mildness." For that reason, histories have gone unwritten. It is better to laugh in a way that makes one's former anxiety merely relative: time (Indus, Prisma, Pontiac . . .) heals all wounds, but not always, not everyone's.

Pray for us.

When the hole has been dug, other women are called up. Among them is my mother; thin as she is, I see her walking away from me as if becoming invisible in the flickering of the fire that surrounds us, and inside me the fear that I may never see her again begins to throb.

"Stay here," she tells me.

(More than three decades later: I have stayed there, I am still standing there, I see myself standing there, I am unable to leave that spot.)

With dozens of other women my mother disappears through the camp gate, but not long afterwards—I begin to sing louder, from relief and joy, and I would have liked to dance but for some reason I cannot—she is back again.

She forms part of a draft team: she and other women are fastened to a rope with which they pull a heavily laden wooden cart into the camp. At the sight of this cart and another one that is being pulled into the square by a second team, the singing stops. Along the sides of the carts flags have been draped, white ones on which, in the center of a white field, stands a graphic sign, red—not a ball, as on the Japanese flag, but a cross. These are Red Cross carts. The women who pull the carts are laughing and shouting gayly to the women who have stayed behind in the square.

Food! The carts are loaded with sacks of rice and potatoes, crates of bread, baskets of fruit, and water—barrels full of water, the war must be over now. There is flour, there is meat, biscuits, chewing gum, coffee, tea, cigarettes, soap, medicines and bandages (I think: might there also be *books?*). Will we all go to our houses now to fetch our pans and cans and boxes and canisters, and will we perhaps be allowed to leave the camp then? Where is my sister? My sister ought to be here now. Where is Nettie Stenvert? Alas, Nettie Stenvert is dead. I saw her two days ago lying like a silver doll with closed eyes in a plywood coffin. Food! Yippee! Yippee! Yay! I wave to my mother with my hat.

What happens next is quite different from what all those women and children are thinking and hoping so passionately.

All the food, all that abundance, must be tipped from the carts into the hole, on orders given by Sone in person. The servants of death pierce and slit the sacks with their sabres or bayonets so that the rice pours down like rain and flour blows away like the calluses one files from one's feet. The servants of death start pissing on the loaves; with their boots the servants of death trample the pineapples, papayas, sawos, bananas and other fruit into a pulp from which a sweet smell arises. The two carts are set on fire with

117

flame throwers, and shoved, burning, into the hole where everything that can burn begins to burn and everything that can carbonize carbonizes.

We stand and watch. My mother, from a distance, signals the command that I must stay where I am and must not do what some women do who run screaming to their deaths by attacking the Jap, or by throwing themselves head first into the hole, embracing the food that lies there with both arms, as their clothes burst into flame.

My mother: what is it about her? It is as if she has grown fatter. As if the Red Cross has also issued breasts, of which she has secretly picked herself a pair from the cart. It is unbelievable, but my mother is laughing, the way she always laughs. Mother most wonderful. Pray for us. Mother most amiable. Pray for us. Mother of divine mercy. Pray for us. Mother of Jeroen Brouwers. Banzai!

Finally, water is poured into the hole, then the red sand is thrown on top of it; over that go new waves of water and new layers of sand, until a bubbling, hissing, gurgling, stinking slush is formed from which stubborn black-red clouds of smoke keep rising as if from an unquenchable, unappeasable hell. The Red Cross has never presented the prisoners at Tjideng with any gifts whatsoever; anyone who asserts that it has will have no proof.

The prisoners at Tjideng get no food and no water for three long days; the Japanese are roaring drunk during those days and behave, for the last time in their war, as insane sadists, and I get lost for good in the labyrinth in which I shall wander for decades trying to find my way, hither and thither, look-who-goes-there, I am looking for my mother.

"Mo"-"ther."

Although she is dead now, I may perhaps find her yet, sometime, somewhere, in the mist, perhaps in my own writings.

Against a background of fire and red-black clouds, my mother comes back to the place where I, on one leg, on my roller skate, have stayed—on her orders. I have not pretended to see something other than what was to be seen; I saw it just as it was, in order to remember it. Among the screaming, wailing, praying, fainting women, my mother comes toward me— as long as I live she will come toward me, there, at that moment, her full breasts swaying. I stretch out my arms to her, I laugh, and my laughter throws a tiny echo against the sounding board formed by the brim of my hat.

Then suddenly, between her who is coming and me—for some reason I cannot move—the camp commandant, Captain Kenichi Sone, with his red frog's head, staggering with drink; each time one of his feet touches the earth a clinking noise springs from his boot. He raises his stick to my mother, and I hear the swish of the stick in the air before it lands so hard upon her that I think she must have been cut in two by the blow. Other Japs rush forward, red and croaking like their leader, and also strike my mother with whatever weapons they have. I hear her screaming. It happens less than five yards from me. I cannot move my feet.

Again: it is not "something else" that happens, and I am not thinking of "something else" but only:

The clothes are torn from my mother's body. She is wearing my dead grandmother's flowered dress, she is wearing a large bra reinforced with whalebone, which bulges more than I have ever seen a bra bulge or ever would see in years to come. If only I could think of something else now, why doesn't something funny occur to me now—for instance; Is it true, that a gnu. . . ." The bra is yanked from my mother's body so that the handsful of rice she had stuffed in the cups fall from her in a rustling cascade and she is breastless as before. Then I see a second shower of rice fall between her feet. Even in her underpants my mother had secreted pounds of rice. The rice grains bounce in all directions over the asphalt.

No, now there will be nothing to laugh at for a long time.

"Those terrible years": With that simple understatement my mother was to describe her camp life in a letter to my father a few months later.

Much later she was to tell me that she had stolen the rice *for me* because I was the last thing she still had.

What am I to do with my "camp syndrome," the remorse that I try to drive away by slapping myself in the face whenever, unexpectedly, film scenes from my life in that camp appear before my eyes?

My mother must have seen this scene at the time of her death. Now I am the one who carries it with me until the hour of my death.

Full of grace, the Lord is with thee, blessed art thou among women and blessed is the fruit of thy womb. . . . Ricketicketick! There goes my grandmother's rosary which my mother wears as a necklace. The black beads bounce away and in the glow of the fire they are as red as the grains of rice.

Prayer. No, I have never known, never understood what that is, unless I have always known and understood that it is nonsense, although the words of many prayers have a poignant beauty, a beauty comparable to "Seresta Forte," "Eldopal Retard," "Pyridoxine Labaz," and "Mogadon."

It is as if the Japs, with their weapons, mean to beat my mother into the ground right through the asphalt. Sone personally kicks her between her legs with his boots that jingle as if there are bells on them, and I witness it personally. Beware, Sone. I am that little boy in the crowd and my eyes nearly pop out as I watch. I personally, Mr. Sone, son of the sun, shall describe your death in three haiku—that is, three times five syllables, seven syllables, five syllables. I shall not need more syllables to chop the memory of you to pieces. I can read, and soon I shall be able to write, you suddenly wear a collar of blood, may the flies come and get you.

My mother bleeds where I came out of her with a head like a cobblestone. I feel her pain between my own legs, as if I myself had received a bayonet thrust in that place; my mother's wounds will have to be stitched up with a curved needle.

Of all these memories the most terrible seems to be this: a few grains of rice still cling to the hair beneath my mother's belly; the Japs laugh as Sone tries to kick them away.

Beware Sone, your head rolls in the mud, as red as the ball on the Japanese flag.

Queen of angels. Queen of patriarchs. Queen of prophets. Queen of apostles. Queen of martyrs. Queen of confessors. Queen of virgins. Queen of all saints. Queen of the immaculate conception. Queen of the most holy rosary. Queen of Peace. Pray for us. Save us. Have mercy upon us. Hear us. Answer us.

It has been recorded: "My mother was the most beautiful mother; at that moment I ceased to love her."

From that moment I lost my way. My distaste for life, my longing not to exist. From that moment I know that I will always prefer to be alone, with no attachment to anyone or anything, for I do not want to see my love and the beauty I cherish destroyed or damaged. At that moment I thought: now I want a different mother, because this one is broken. As dec-ades later, standing by the table where they were busy repairing the damage to the body of my beloved, beautiful wife with a sickle-shaped needle, I thought: Now I want a different wife.

Liza!

(That sometimes, in the days after my mother's death, I pressed the telephone receiver against my fly until I saw red before my eyes, and screamed, "Croak croak!")

We won't leave each other, will we mamma? Will we? Will we mamma?

This I think, while I am still standing where my mother told me to stand, although I would have liked to fly to her with outstretched arms, throwing bombs, brum brum, tets tets, splattering the glass dome of my cockpit with blood, my mother's own Danny, of whom she can be *proud,* his hat is his halo: holy, three times holy is he, Danny the writer, Danny who can no longer laugh.

But my one foot is heavier than the other: so immensely heavy that I cannot move from the place where I have been standing for hours, first in the sun and then among the burning houses.

Small wonder: my roller skate has sunk into the molten asphalt and is stuck fast, immovable, so that the whole world hangs from my right foot.

I must stand and watch, immobile, while my face drips away from me with weeping.

In the woods near my home, where I ended up after driving around for hours, I stood among the all-enveloping shrouds of spider web in the mist. Not immobile; I was trembling all over. My knees, my jaws, especially my hands, and even the skin of my skull seemed to be shaking.

I was deep in the wood, far from the paths and tracks that I had left without taking my bearings or noticing where I was walking. I had come to a lake. The water was black, but in the middle floated an island of brittle ice that was turning into water again. I could not see the lower parts of the trees on the opposite shore, where the mist had piled up into statues and tombs. Everything was stage scenery, or was becoming stage scenery. Nothing moved if you did not look carefully, and nothing was audible if you were not listening. But through the apparently motionless water small ripples ran for no particular reason. The almost imperceptible moisture that came down touched not only the water but me as well, my face and my remaining hair. And what could be heard was a deep-toned non-sound or un-sound, coming from far away, as if caused in "time" or in "history," as if somewhere in that existing-nonexisting ghost world a chord had been struck.

This was a good place to commemorate, all alone, my feet sinking into the wet, rotting leaves, the annihilation of my mother's body.

May the angels lead her into paradise.

This paradise my mother must have imagined as "tempo dahulu," the good old colonial times in the "Indies" before the Japanese invasion. We had a house in town and a house in the mountains, my mother was eternal youth and eternal beauty, and her husband was reasonably well-off; we had a host of servants in both houses, we had our own swimming pool, we had a car, we had a movie camera. What is left of all that is preserved on films made at the time, but these films can not be projected by the modernized, improved equipment of the years after "tempo dahulu," equipment chiefly of Japanese manufacture, so that the recorded images were forgotten forever, as if they had never been recorded.

May the martyrs receive thee and lead thee into the holy city. May the choir of angels receive thee, and mayest thou have eternal rest. Aeternam habeas requiem.

At exactly 3:00 P.M., when my mother, at the other end of the country, hundreds of kilometers away, went to dust like a diamond in the flames, I drew in lungsful of fog.

I said: "Ketemu lagi, mamma," be prosperous, be happy.

And as I said it I smiled, as always, and I imagined that my mother, wherever she was, floating along in the river of souls heard me and smiled too, as she,

my brave mother, friendly pelican, in spite of her pain and the blood that dripped from her body, smiled at me when I, having at last freed myself from my roller skate, crouched by her side on the scalding asphalt—at an epicentre of world history, August 1945. I would have wished to cleanse her and refresh her with bits of cloth, with water and scent. I was prepared to exchange my most precious possession, my Danny book, for a splash of water, and my second most precious possession, my hat, for anything else, ointment, oil, a bit of bandage. But no one had anything that could be deemed even as precious as a dog-eared children's book and a worn, dirty, smelly topi. With my hat I fanned coolness to my mother and I stroked her shorn head. I kept watch by her, after first gathering the remains of her flowered dress, her bra and her underpants; the remains of the rosary I left where they were. You aren't going to die, are you mamma? No, of course not, darling. And then, in order to pretend that something other was happening than what was happening, and in order to conjure up scenes before my mother's eyes that were less terrible than the scenes of which we ourselves were a part, I read to her from my book. I needed no light for it, although the glow of the fire hung like a red haze over the pages—I knew the book by heart. *Danny goes on a trip.* "By Leonard Roggeveen." "Look-who-goes-there. There goes Danny." Wherever a page was missing, I made up the story myself, as befits a writer-to-

126

be. Then, as I turned a page for form's sake, my father's photograph fell on my mother. "My dearest Sjoekie, Though I prayed to Our Lady every day with the little ones for Daddy's safe return . . . and now our prayer has been answered. We may be thankful indeed. . . ."

Tabé mamma. Meanwhile I have made good progress with my reading. Only the books I write myself I never read once they are published; I need not remember the things I have written. Go from me now—I no longer need to remember you either. I am "not nice," I am "hard" and "bitter," I am "unfeeling." I am sick with hatred, hatred of life, of people, of women. I am sick with fear. No one can get through to me. Hear me. Answer me. Pray for me. Have mercy upon me.

Ketemu lagi.

When, at 3:00, I held my watch, which I could hear ticking in the silence, close to my face, and the mist poured into me and I imagined how my mother's body became again what it had been seventy-two or seventy-three years ago—"the same" and yet "not the same," that is how the world is composed—there happened:

Nothing.

No roe deer with golden eyes suddenly appeared to me, standing among the statues and tombs of mist on the other side of the water; and no flock of blackbirds alighted to sing for me with my mother's voice, bringing me a message from her; not even a pine needle fell in the water, to float about in a special way so that, in its thin wake a magic word became legible, a word that, uttered aloud, would heal my soul.

The wind did not suddenly pass by, coming from somewhere, on its way to somewhere else.

The trellis of spider webs did not break, the mist did not suddenly vanish, the moisture did not cease to descend, nor were the thousands of frogs' eggs and flies' eggs not laid in the corruption of the rotting leaves in which I was standing, to be hatched when it was May and summer again.

I thought, but without feeling anything:

"At Eikelenburg Crematorium, 7 Eikelenburglaan in Rijswijk, at 3 o'clock. Following the cremation, condolences may be offered in the reception room at the crematorium."

"The many tokens of sympathy on the death of our beloved mother have moved us deeply. We wish to express our heartfelt gratitude."

In the mist. Past the halfway point in my life, just before the intermission. Written in a trembling hand.

Nor, as I desired so passionately, did Liza emerge from the wings, after my mother had left the stage, dressed in the same delicate blue as my mother had worn on her last journey, and though I could see Liza's loveliness and the gold of her body where it was golden, and the diamond of her body and the sunken

128

red of her body where I know it to be sunken red. Morning star. Refuge of the sick. Comforter of the afflicted.

That I should pull my feet free from the sucking ground and walk towards her, look-tinkle-who-tin-kle-goes-tinkle-there, as if years had not passed, as if things had not been definitively fixed in their places, and anything could still happen. Come, hand in hand, in our splendid robes of silk, lace and ermine, we form the center of a festive procession, we walk on soft carpets, we pass through lanes of honor and under triumphal arches, we are bestrewn with flowers—the angels will lead us into paradise.

Oh Liza. Bye bye, Liza.

Return, O my soul, to thy rest.

That she might smilingly kneel before me, and open up my clothes with soft fingers and then, with her mouth, with her tongue, with her hands, with caresses of her soft hair, with sweet words, with gentle, crooning incantations, with oh—

Make soft the calluses that grow all over my body.

I drove home, I sat down at my desk to resume, apparently untouched, unmoved, unperturbed, my work on the book about suicide in Dutch literature. But I could not see; my face was dripping away from me in porridge-like lumps, the skin of my forehead slithered into my eyes, the skin of my nose and cheeks fell like a melting substance onto the papers that lay on the desk in front of me: the chapter on the suicide of Jacob Hiegentlich. In the margin of this manuscript it says: 1.26. Gerrit Verrips here. Three pages further: 1.27.81. My mother is dead. The chapter on Hiegentlich, who like me was born on the 30th of April, and who committed suicide in the year of my birth, the war year 1940, ends with these lines:

"If Hiegentlich had survived the war and had been able to celebrate his thirty-eighth birthday on Monday, April 30, 1945, he would have learnt that at half-past three that afternoon Hitler took his own life by shooting himself with a revolver.

On that day I was five—unaware of Hiegentlich, but already aware of Hitler, and also of death."

In order to take myself out of myself, in order to cover and smother my fear with wads of mist, I began to drink gin.

Trembling, I just managed to pour the gin into a tumbler, but I could not raise the glass to my mouth without sloshing the contents over the rim. To control the trembling of my hand I had to fetch a tea towel from the kitchen, hang it around my neck and stick the thumb of the hand holding and raising the glass through the loop by which the tea towel had been hanging from its hook on the wall.

Pulling the other end of the cloth down along my neck with the other hand, I was able to hoist the hand with the glass to my mouth and take the first few sips without spilling too much. As soon as I had swallowed them, the trembling stopped and the glass stayed where it was without any further help.

Around me was the safe house, the house, perhaps in which I shall soon die, in this same chair, at the same desk. Elsewhere in the house my wife is busy with the little girl. Nothing exists that does not touch something else, but what am I to do with it? What has it to do with me? What must I feel? On the television there was "Telebingo II." "A program of quizzes and entertainment for charity. First prize: a car. With the co-operation of well-known celebrities who will press the buttons, and top variety artists from home and abroad. Presented by Mies Bouwman." Around the house stood the trees, shrubs and hedges of my garden, like stage props between me and the world. They must never go away. House and garden lay under a glass dome of mist. In my study I saw myself reflected as if I were outside in the mist, led out of myself and my fears, looking myself in the face.

What time of night is it?

I heard my wrist watch ticking. It is a Certina. Automatic. Club 2000. Swiss made. It is one of those watches that do not have to be wound as long as you wear it on your wrist and as long as your pulse beats. It is a watch with a calendar.

Later the wind rose and raindrops appeared on the outside of the window, slowly sliding across the pane so that between me and my other self a web-like lattice formed and I saw my face dissolve into liquid in the mist.

"Louwhoek," Exel
January 30–May 2, 1981

131